A COUNTRY
NOT
CONSIDERED

OTHER BOOKS BY TOM WAYMAN

Poetry

Waiting for Wayman 1973

For and against the Moon: Blues, Yells, and Chuckles 1974

Money and Rain: Tom Wayman Live! 1975

Free Time 1977

A Planet Mostly Sea 1979

Living on the Ground: Tom Wayman Country 1980

Introducing Tom Wayman 1980

The Nobel Prize Acceptance Speech 1981

Counting the Hours: City Poems 1983

The Face of Jack Munro 1986

In a Small House on the Outskirts of Heaven 1989

Essays

Inside Job: Essays on the New Work Writing 1983

Editor

Beaton Abbot's Got the Contract 1974

A Government Job at Last 1976

Going for Coffee 1981

East of Main (with Calvin Wharton) 1989

Paperwork 1991

A COUNTRY
NOT
CONSIDERED

Canada, Culture, Work

TOM WAYMAN

For Frances —
who considers
ALL
things!
Many thanks
Tom

Anansi

First published in 1993 by
House of Anansi Press Limited
1800 Steeles Avenue West
Concord, Ontario
L4K 2P3
(416) 445-3333

Canadian Cataloguing in Publication Data

Wayman, Tom, 1945 -
A country not considered: Canada, culture, work

ISBN 0-88784-538-X

1. Canadian literature (English) — History and
criticism.*   2. Canadian poetry (English) — History
and criticism.*   3. Canada — Civilization.*
I. Title.

PS8071.W38 1993   C810'.54   C93-093588-8
PR9189.6.W38 1993

Cover Concept: Angel Guerra
Cover Design and Photograph: Brant Cowie/ArtPlus Limited
Typesetting: Tony Gordon Ltd.

Printed and bound in Canada

House of Anansi Press gratefully acknowledges the
support of the Canada Council, Ontario Ministry of
Culture, Tourism, and Recreation, Ontario Arts
Council, and Ontario Publishing Centre in the
development of writing and publishing in Canada.

Contents

ACKNOWLEDGEMENTS

Essays here were first presented (often in slightly different versions) at various occasions and in various publications, to whose organizers and editors I am grateful.

"Laramie or Squamish: What Use Is Canadian Culture?" was published in *Border/Lines* (York University), No. 14 (Winter 1988-89). The essay is based on a lecture given at the University of Winnipeg in October 1987 as part of my duties as writer-in-residence. "A House without Books: The Writer in Canadian Society" was a talk presented at a Soviet – Canadian conference on "Writers in Their Society" at Castlegar, B.C., in March 1989. "A House without Books" subsequently appeared in *Canadian Literature*, No. 130 (Autumn 1991). An abridged version of "Marty and Zieroth: Two Writers from Elsewhere" has been accepted for publication in *Canadian Literature*.

"Fighter in Amber: An Appreciation of Milton Acorn" was published in *Canadian Dimension*, Vol. 21, No. 4 (July/August 1987). "The Skin of the Earth: My Neruda" was a lecture given to the Humanities Institute of Douglas College, New Westminster, B.C., in March 1987; the essay was published in *Event*, Vol. 17, No. 3 (Fall 1988). "An Aspirin as Big as the Sun: Poetry and Politics" was an address to the Federation of B.C. Writers annual convention in April 1989 in White Rock, B.C. "An Aspirin as Big as the Sun" was published in *Quarry*, Vol. 39, No. 4 (Fall 1990).

"Visible Consequences, Invisible Jobs" appeared in *Paperwork: Contemporary Poems from the Job* (Madeira Park, B.C.: Harbour, 1991). "Split Shift and After: Some Issues of the New Work Writing" was published in *Poetry Canada Review*, Vol. 9, No. 3 (Summer 1988). "Sitting by the Grave of Literary Ambition: Where I Am Now in My Writing" was published in *Event* Vol. 20, No. 1 (Spring 1991).

Concepts here originated and were modified through conversation and correspondence with many individuals over the years. I particularly appreciate the salutary effects on my ideas of the viewpoints of members of the Vancouver Industrial Writers' Union, the Kootenay School of Writing's Vancouver Centre, the Vancouver General Membership Branch of the IWW. Whether affiliated or not to organizations or institutions that are meaningful to me, my friends and family — and their lives — have always been my touchstone for evaluating the content of what I write. I want to acknowledge with thanks their contribution to my life and art.

Every effort has been made to contact copyright holders. In the event of an inadvertent omission or error, the publisher should be notified at House of Anansi Press, 1800 Steeles Avenue West, Concord, Ontario, Canada L4K 2P3. The following publishers and authors have generously given permission to quote entire poems:

Kenneth Rexroth: *Selected Poems.* Copyright © 1951 by Kenneth Rexroth. Reprinted by permission of New Directions Publishing Corp.

Poems by Sid Marty reprinted by permission of the author.

Poems by Dale Zieroth reprinted by permission of the author.

"Lazybones" and "To the Foot from Its Child" from *Extravagaria* by Pablo Neruda. Translation copyright © 1974 by Alastair Reid. Reprinted by permission of Farrar, Straus, and Giroux, Inc.

A COUNTRY
NOT
CONSIDERED

INTRODUCTION:
A COUNTRY NOT
CONSIDERED

We never claimed to know precisely when the birth of this New Consciousness would take place, or what assortment of potions might be required to initiate contractions, but as to the birthplace we had always taken it for granted that this shining nativity would happen here, *out of the ache of our American labor.*

Europe was too stiff to bring it off, Africa too primitive, China too poor. And the Russians thought they had already accomplished it. But Canada? Canada had never even been considered.

KEN KESEY, *The Demon Box*

I was born, grew up, and have lived most of my life in a country that many of my fellow citizens, as well as a person as culturally aware as the U.S. author Ken Kesey, regard as beneath consideration as a locale for new and significant ideas, of new hope for the human species. The present book is an exploration of life in a country not considered.

I have chosen three provinces or states (of mind) of that country to focus on, although the boundaries between these three concerns keep shifting: Canadian culture, literature (especially contemporary poetry), and daily work. In my experience none of these areas of attention are judged by the surrounding society as having any real potential to create that "shining nativity" of which Kesey speaks. Why I disagree is the substance of my writing here.

I begin with Canada and its culture. I live on an estate in the Selkirk Mountains of southeastern British Columbia about fifty-eight kilometres outside the town of Nelson, and I make my living teaching imaginative writing (locally and elsewhere). When people ask me what possible use gaining skills in such writing could be, I talk about Nelson. In 1986 the movie *Roxanne,* starring Steve Martin, was filmed in Nelson. This successful remake of the Cyrano de Bergerac tale made extensive use of Nelson's picturesque mountain setting and the town's many 1890s-era heritage buildings. But when the movie was made, the locale was changed from Nelson, B.C., to an imaginary Nelson south of the line in Washington State, U.S.A. The touches were small: the U.S. flag was raised over the Nelson firehall (focus of much of the action of the film), and U.S.-style mailboxes replaced Canada Post's during filming in the streets. But the import of such changes is enormous: what occurs in a remote mountain town in Washington is viewed by cultural tastemakers, and hence audiences, as culturally significant. The same story set in a remote mountain town in B.C. is not.

So my reply to those who question the value of learning creative writing skills centres on the issue of self-identity and, ultimately, self-confidence. If we do not articulate for ourselves what our lives are like, no one is going to do it for us. At best what we have or what we have achieved will be co-opted and presented back to us as the possession or accomplishment of somebody else. *Unless* we articulate our lives we will forever be seen by others, and ultimately by ourselves, as insignificant, not *worthy* of consideration.

Regarding ourselves as insignificant can lead to some bizarre practices. I have a friend who teaches at a community college in Cranbrook, B.C., a town one mountain range east of here in the Rocky Mountain trench. East of Cranbrook the majestic peaks of the Rockies provide an ever-present backdrop to life in that town; these are mountains that make even the summits and ridges of the Southern Selkirks that surround Nelson look puny.

But in the literal shadow of these giants, which form the roof of our country and continent, many of the Cranbrook college students trudge to class dressed in what they believe Californians wear. Even through the deep snow and cold of an East Kootenay winter, the students insist on showing up on campus in beach attire. My friend calls them "Cranbrook surfers." Entertainment, advertising, and all other mainstream cultural and commercial artifacts that barrage young people insist that such clothes are what significant human beings wear. It is understandable that students choose to make themselves ridiculous by adopting such wildly inappropriate garb. But that young people do so is simultaneously comic and sad. Yet the "Cranbrook surfers" are only a very visible manifestation of the way a lack of self-confidence in who we are, in where and how we live, diminishes our self-respect. Culturally speaking, it was the filmmakers who shifted Nelson to Washington State, but it is the young people of Cranbrook who have moved that town to California. And yet, in physical reality, each town remains in its own unique mountain setting.

The aspect of culture that I am most familiar with is literature, and so this is the second area of the unconsidered country I try to map in my writing here. An accurate examination of the economic status of authors provides just one bit of evidence of the lack of regard the general population has for reading. Why the public should assess reading as unworthy of consideration, except in hopes of escape from daily life, is a question I try to probe. Although some partisans of the Canadian book industry continue to insist Canadians buy more books per capita than citizens of this or that other place, anyone who teaches English or writing knows how dubious these statistics are in practice. What *sort* of books do Canadians buy? What *sort* of books do Canadians read? Certainly this alleged interest in books doesn't apply to literature, to judge from our students.

I find people are often astonished when I tell how even our writing students display a deep-rooted antipathy to reading. These students want to be writers, but not readers. I can harangue them about how no one learning to compose or perform music would refuse to listen to as many recordings and attend as many concerts as she or he possibly could — to assess the best *and* the worst.

Nobody seriously studying art would refuse to go to galleries, and pore over reproductions, in search of technical and inspirational information about their genre. But something has so influenced our writing students concerning literature that they perpetually balk at reading.

A few years ago I was responding in a first-year college class of mine to a student who was writing fiction well but did not know the conventions ordinarily used in English to present direct quotation, dialogue. Since others in the class had demonstrated some uncertainty in this technique, as well, I did a little presentation of the use of quotation marks and so on. Then I began to explain that if they found my exposition of the conventions confusing, there was a model readily available they could copy. It had been my intention to suggest they use daily newspaper reports as the source to see how dialogue is ordinarily indicated in English. But I was interrupted before I could get beyond my remark about how there exists an easily accessible model they could copy. "You mean," one student blurted out, her voice changing to a tone of absolute contempt, "read a *book?*" Startled by her obvious vehement dislike of such repulsive objects, I hastened to assure her it was newspapers, newspapers that I had in mind.

Yet it is in that pariah province of literature that more helpful information than how to use quotation marks may be found. I argue that Canadian literature potentially can provide some of that sense of self-worth denied us by much in the surrounding commercial and cultural environment. And I try to show why self-assurance is necessary to the health of a community. Not just because we might wince at a judgement of Canada like Kesey's, or at the sight of some of our young people costumed as surfers eight hundred kilometres from the nearest ocean. Self-confidence is vital because the sense that each of us is a significant member of a community is the foundation of democracy. For if we do not think our lives *matter* much in the larger sphere of life, why would we believe we have any right to participate in influencing the world that surrounds us?

I say literature has this *potential,* because I express in some of this book an ambivalence towards the provinces I am mapping. I see what might be found here and describe how what exists so far differs from what could be. But my criticisms — of Canadian culture, of literature — are made in hope, not despair. I believe there are no parts of any unconsidered country that humanity can write off as forever condemned to irrelevance, to insignificance.

One region closest to my heart, although I know it is furthest from being regarded as significant by nearly every other citizen, is that area of literature called contemporary poetry. In my life I have found this to be a district rich in treasures of every kind — emotional, political, comic, domestic, ecological, interpersonal, and more. But I am conscious that most people's experiences with poems in school and afterwards lead them to regard poetry, even more than literature generally, as a desert at best and a torture centre at worst. Far from being a locale whose inhabitants gain self-confidence from their sojourn there, poetry for a majority of people in our society is one more place that makes them feel stupid, unworthy, small.

I know poetry does not have to produce this effect. And where a population regards an art form as significant, the artists gain self-confidence, and flourish. Chile, for instance, with a population smaller than English-speaking Canada's, has been awarded two Nobel Prizes for poetry since 1945. In this book I try to show some of the delight and insight certain kinds of poetry have provided me. Displaying as always that ambivalence towards my subjects, though, I also probe some issues concerning this poetry that I feel are important.

Interwoven throughout my look at poetry, at literature, at culture, at Canada, is my response to the third province with which this book is concerned — daily work. My thesis here can be boiled down to two statements: an accurate portrayal of daily employment is nowhere found in our culture, and — or *because* — we are not free at work.

To me these propositions are central to understanding and to depicting our national, artistic, personal existence. I attempt to show the interconnectedness of this viewpoint with most other topics here. In demonstrating the implications of these two statements on work, I confess I sometimes feel like those women at the start of the current incarnation of the women's movement who observed that, after they contributed to any discussion in a mixed group of men and women, the conversation resumed at the point where the last male had spoken. Few people want to dispute that an accurate depiction of the central daily experience of Canadians is absent from our culture. And few people want to dispute that work is an undemocratic experience shaping our lives in the midst of a supposedly democratic society. But few people also seem willing to pursue what these facts mean.

Theorists of family dysfunction now talk about how a major harmful effect of such dysfunction — alcoholism or child abuse, for example — is the *denial* that the problem invariably involves. That is, the theorists maintain that no matter how horrible or slight the dysfunction, the problem is greatly exacerbated by the denial that surrounds it. The child or other family members cannot deal with the problem because no one will admit the problem exists. Indeed, young people frequently become disoriented due to the double consciousness such denial involves: the problem is obviously present, but everyone around the child behaves as though there is no problem. So the child is taught that what she or he knows and feels is false, and that what she or he is aware is untrue is real. This dysfunction is not a good basis on which to build self-worth, self-esteem, a sense of personal significance. Instead family members of all ages must adopt the most elaborate and bizarre possible activities and rationales to protect the denial. The result of such a process is long-term harm not only to the person with the problem but to all members of the family.

I argue here that the lack of democracy, the lack of freedom, at work is a community dysfunction. How can people behave sanely in their lives, ricocheting in their time awake between eight hours where they are expected to be responsible adult citizens and parents, and eight hours where they are expected to be respectfully, unquestioningly, childishly obedient to arbitrary authority? I try to show ways in which the denial of this situation harms ourselves and our young people. In various essays I also try to demonstrate how ending this denial would enhance our community, artistic, and personal lives.

As with a consciousness of women's subservient position in society, an awareness of how unfreedom at work each day influences our community and ourselves cannot be unlearned. On the planet at present the inhabitants of many nations are demanding independence for their ethnic, religious, or language group. And that is well and good. But after the shouting or the shooting stops, on the morning after the victory celebrations whether deep in Eastern Europe or in Quebec, most people will file back through the office door or factory gate to a condition of servitude. The person who controls them there may now be of the same ethnic or religious or linguistic background as themselves. But the humiliation will continue. To me it is no wonder that the citizens of newly independent states often quickly feel cheated, wronged, shortchanged, and turn on one another in civil wars or search out some scapegoat from among their fellow citizens on which to place the blame for the lack of freedom they still feel. This is the price of denial of the central fact of political and personal life.

Such a denial leads to some odd cultural consequences, too. I remember attending the Canadian Booksellers Association national convention in Vancouver in 1986. There the publishers' displays were laid out in a huge hall. I recall wandering up and down aisle after aisle after aisle, staring at books on nearly every imaginable topic: biographies of generals and entrepreneurs and sports stars, cookbooks of many exotic cuisines, popularizations of the latest scientific theories, self-help tomes on dozens of matters from plumbing to divorce, travel tales from pole to pole and accounts of adventure from mountain climbing to descents into the deepest abysses of the oceans. What was completely absent was *any* book on the experience that governs most Canadians' daily lives: our work.

Where reviewers confront cultural products that focus on employment, the need to maintain this denial is often paramount. For example, although reviews of my anthologies of contemporary U.S. and Canadian work poetry are frequently positive, the negative ones invariably try to argue that an examination of daily work is not a suitable topic for culture. Why should we have to read, asked one newspaper reviewer of my most recent anthology, *Paperwork* (1991), "about a reality from which we try, vicariously or otherwise, to escape?" The reviewer quoted William Faulkner as stating that since work is the only activity people do for eight hours a day, no wonder people are so miserable.

Yet if the central experience of each day is so boring, and makes us so miserable, would it not follow that art would be the perfect place to assess what happens on the job? After all, the arts are usually touted as humanity's way of exploring existence, of expressing what it means to be human. In fact, the new writing about work in no way describes work as simply boring or miserable. Instead it depicts the workplace as a locale where the entire range of human emotions is found — not excluding boredom and misery, but also including accomplishment, danger, joy, humour, rage, romanticism, whimsy, inquisitiveness, and much, much more. How could it be otherwise, since the job site is a place where human beings gather each day to live, interact, produce, in fact, re-create the entire society? The new work writing shows that the range of personalities at work, and of responses to the job, are as wide as humanity itself. I am convinced that only somebody with a need to cling to a denial of what actually occurs on the job could attempt to reduce such a significant human experience to "boring" and "miserable."

Another negative review tactic is to agree with the premise and then quickly blur the topic. A West Coast English professor had this to say about *Paperwork:*

> I find Wayman's contention that our jobs "form the central and governing core of our lives" a rather sad comment on contemporary society. I feel that poetry has a responsibility to be concerned with the emotional, spiritual, cultural, historical and psychological needs of human beings and that these are the things that most deeply affect both human beings and the human soul.

Presumably because this task is the correct one for poetry, the reviewer reported that "why the daily grind of life on the line should be celebrated and anthologized in . . . poetry remains a mystery to me."

Who could disagree that poetry, like every other art, "has a responsibility to be concerned with the emotional, spiritual, cultural, historical and psychological needs of human beings"? Yet "the emotional, spiritual, cultural, historical and psychological needs of human beings" are not things that come in the mail. Why should art not depict the ways in which the central and governing experience of our lives shapes, for better or worse, such human needs?

I understand, however, that the behavioural pattern of denial does not end the moment someone points out this pattern to those who have adopted it. Sadly some severe personal emotional trauma seems to be the catalyst for a change in behavioural patterns. What the political or cultural equivalent of this trauma is I do not know. My intention with the present book, therefore, is not to convince but to try to state as clearly as possible my assessment of these provinces of our country not considered.

Yet I am aware that clarity or accessibility are not necessarily regarded as virtues in critical writing. When one of these essays was submitted to a cultural magazine, a member of the editorial board telephoned me with the good news that the piece was accepted. He went on to say, though, that the board had found the piece "too clear," almost like a speech. He said that as an editor he tried to use as a criterion of judgement whether or not his father would be able to understand an article. His father was not a literary person. The trouble with my article was that "even my father would be able to understand it."

I was staggered by these comments. "You mean," I floundered, "you'd like me to . . . uh, sort of . . . obscure up the piece a little?" "Not exactly," the reply came. "But, you know, please think about what I've said."

When I had time to consider the matter, I wrote back to say in my defence that the accessibility of my piece was a consequence of who my intended audience is. That is, I see myself as talking to a general public rather than a specialized one. I confessed that I do read my prose pieces out loud before judging them finished. I want to be confident that if I was reading my article aloud face-to-face with someone, there would be nothing that would harm my attempt to communicate as directly as possible with him or her. One aim of my writing, I wrote the editor,

> is to demystify the world: to demystify what happens to us on the job, to demystify the process of artistic creation, to demystify culture and cultural criticism. This calls, as I see it, for speaking with the utmost clarity. This is why I so much admire the writers about science who make very complex ideas available to a much broader audience than the handful of specialists to whom those ideas formerly were limited. If these writers can successfully present startling and difficult concepts concerning the origins of the universe, cosmic strings, or the atmosphere of Saturn to a general public, I believe it is possible to write equally comprehensibly about culture.

I asked what was lost if "even" his father could understand an article. What is so bad about giving his father access to a discussion of cultural matters? My intention, I said, was not to shut people out of such debates but to include them.

> I believe the aim of criticism is to empower people to understand what is happening to them and to help them to participate in changing their environment to suit their own needs and desires.

> The opposite approach to critical writing — overuse of unexplained jargon, the thunder of names being dropped, the employment of needlessly confused or fuzzy sentences — is counterproductive. For example, what is gained by writing obscurely about questions of cultural criticism? Talking among ourselves, we may use jargon, or references to certain other

cultural artifacts, as a kind of shortcut to skip quickly over issues on which we agree in order to get on to a more detailed discussion about other matters. But when we use excessive jargon or other mystified language in an article which is to appear in *public,* we slam doors in people's faces.

I acknowledged that making cultural studies seem difficult or obscure, requiring the existence of cultural specialists to sort issues out, does ensure academic jobs for a handful of people. But there are harmful effects of this practice, too.

When cultural study is mystified, it discourages people who have begun to consider examining their cultural surroundings from continuing their investigations. It implies the assessment of culture is the preserve of an elite and not a suitable activity for ordinary people like you, me or your dad. I think this is wrong since I believe self-awareness of *all* aspects of our surroundings is essential to democracy.

I concluded by describing a "trickle-down" theory of knowledge that I have heard to justify such mystifications. This theory argues that if specialists are allowed to pursue their mysterious trade in well-paid isolation, then the knowledge thus gained will be passed on in some way to ordinary women and men. But in my experience there is precious little that ever trickles down. For instance, I wrote the editor, there has been a mushrooming of experts on linguistics, semiotics, and communications theory who insist they have an enhanced understanding of how language works.

Yet in the normal course of the daily struggle, as we sit down to compose our union leaflets, pamphlets, picket signs, where are all these experts, this language elite? They may well have made discoveries about how language functions that would make our task easier, our use of language more effective. But there is no tangible evidence that this is true. They are not here with us, nor have the insights gained while, say, writing essays on deconstruction of eighteenth-century texts trickled down to those of us forced to use language in the everyday present to protect ourselves from those who would hurt us, from those who attack our quality of life.

The response of the magazine editor to all this was to accept my article as written and to apologize. He explained he was in graduate school, and that, for him, the

> danger of graduate work is that at times I find myself lured into demanding "more sophistication" of certain types of writing when what I'm really asking for — and here's the danger — is some sense of exclusivity. And that's where I have to keep on my toes about the university system: it's too easy to fall into a kind of clubby elitism. Paradoxically, it is by tacitly encouraging that kind of elitism that more than a few academics feel their work is worthwhile.

This generous reaction to my attempt to defend accessibility is only one end of a spectrum, though. At the other end is the accusation that to speak clearly is to be anti-intellectual. In the November/December 1991 issue of *The American Poetry Review,* for example, a letter to the editor complains about the obscurity of a previously published review of the poet Susan Howe. The letter asks for an explanation of what the reviewer meant by the sentence:

> Moving outward from the disjunctive and messianic temporality, as well as double-genderedness, implied in the minister's first name, Howe does not assume her relation to this history, but rather sees it as a systematic practice unpacking the conditions of system.

The reviewer, invited by the editors to reply, offers a description of what she meant by this sentence. Her description would, I think, be understandable by anyone. In order to express herself clearly she takes fourteen centimetres of column space rather than the four centimetres of the confusing sentence. The reviewer defends herself by stating, concerning her explanation of her earlier sentence:

> It would take a very long time for me to write in this way and, frankly, I think it would insult the intelligence of most readers. *The American Poetry Review* pays reviewers by the page: I already feel rather guilty for taking up so much space with this letter.

The reviewer then goes on to accuse the letter writer of holding the general public in "low estimation," because the correspondent asks that the review be comprehensible. The reviewer's reply ends with the further accusation that the letter writer must be anti-intellectual.

I believe what we have here is plain, old-fashioned human defensiveness: when we are shown an error we have made, we often attack. The reviewer begins by implying you are stupid if you cannot understand her review; to have to explain herself clearly would be to "insult the intelligence of most readers." Then the reviewer moves on to the accusations that the letter writer must regard the public as inferior and is, in any case, anti-intellectual. The reviewer's *defence* of her obscurity — that clarity would take too long for her to write, and that it would prove too costly for the magazine — needs no comment.

The use of specialized language, jargon undecipherable to the uninitiated, is not limited to academia. Every trade has its own names for things, as discussed in this book in "Split Shift and After: Some Issues of the New Work Writing." But in most trades jargon is not often used as a means of concealing the work that is going on, nor is it used to make the uninitiated feel unworthy or foolish. In my experience if a craftsperson is explaining his or her job, or observations about the job, to an outsider, the craftsperson is only too happy to interpret any jargon he or she may have inadvertently used. The craftsperson does not think you have low intelligence for not understanding these terms, nor does he or she complain about the time and cost of communicating clearly to you what he or she meant. I do not believe using jargon as a screen to keep the uninitiated from understanding what is being said is a required characteristic for being an intellectual. Clarity is not synonymous with simplicity or one-dimensionality of thought.

To be regarded as special appears to be a human need, however, and perhaps the resistance to clarity that the gatekeepers of culture often express reflects this desire to be part of a unique group. Changes in my own life have led me to examine the emotional roots of many of my *own* ideas, and that is the substance of the final essay in this book. Such personal explorations seem to me now to be essential for understanding the dimensions of the self, for the ways the self functions in the world. I have come to believe that if one's personal behaviour is an unconsidered country, no amount of insights into the external world will bring the rewards we seek in life. Why, as a species and as individuals, do we continue to try to understand more and more about existence? Why do we struggle towards that "New Consciousness," the "shining nativity" that Kesey speaks of? I think it is because we sense our individual and collective lives could be better than they are. But what do we mean by "better"? There are personal and familial roots for our definition of "better," no less than community and national ones. I do not feel we have understood the provinces of any country until we have explored, in addition, the basis of our own personal behaviours as we travel through these provinces, and through time. I believe I, and my country, and its culture, are worth such consideration.

1 LARAMIE OR SQUAMISH: WHAT USE IS CANADIAN CULTURE?

When free trade with the U.S. is denounced, or when cutbacks in government funding of the arts are opposed, one issue invariably raised is the threat to Canadian culture. Yet in such a discussion the *value* of Canadian culture is often accepted as a given, or is alluded to only briefly. The question of how useful our culture is to our society has never seemed that simple to me. I find the commonly given explanations as to why Canadian culture has worth are unconvincing at best and transparently false at worst. I do believe Canadian culture has merit. Determining what is valuable about our culture is a tricky matter, however, as I hope to show in what follows.

Before I continue, though, let me be more precise about what I mean by "culture." An article by Ian McKay in Memorial University's *Labor/Le Travailleur* a number of years ago (8/9, 1981-82) pointed out there are nearly three hundred definitions for the word in current use (for instance, "logging camp culture," "women's culture," et cetera). I intend to refer here to a nonanthropological sense of the word. By "Canadian culture" I mean those artifacts produced by Canadians that are commonly referred to as part of the fine arts, performing arts, literary arts, and so on.

To begin to assess the worth of Canadian culture, I have to note English-speaking Canada's history as a cultural colony, first of England and then the United States. Such a past has resulted in many of us being affected by culture in strange ways. I was giving a talk in 1987 to a class at Vancouver Technical Secondary School. The teacher of this English class had chosen, despite the approved curriculum, to present her students with a whole term of contemporary poetry about Vancouver. I told the class how lucky they were to have this still-rare opportunity. When I was growing up in British Columbia in the 1950s and 1960s, the culture I was aware of was entirely produced by and about people who lived elsewhere — either geographically or in time. Thus, for example, we learned poetry was written by dead Englishmen. And as for the culture we were exposed to outside of school, the idea of a rock and roll star being based in Vancouver was unthinkable.

I described for the class my own experience of driving from Vancouver to California for the first time in 1966, and how when I initially drove into Los Angeles I felt that I was at last present in a real place. Of course, I knew Vancouver was real. But I was tremendously excited to be among the place names that I had so often heard mentioned in books and songs, or seen in movies. To be heading at high speed down the freeway, past the signs for Hollywood Boulevard, La Cienega Boulevard, Sunset Boulevard, was, for me, to have finally arrived on the planet Earth.

And I did not gain much sense of perspective, I informed the class, until a couple of years later when I took a job in northern Colorado as a university instructor. The town where I taught, Fort Collins, is close to Laramie, Wyoming. Since Laramie is the setting for, or referred to in, a number of western stories, movies, cowboy ballads, and so on, I was anxious to see the place. Yet when I finally visited, I was shocked to discover that it appeared to be a small town, not much bigger than, say, Squamish, at the head of Howe Sound, north of Vancouver. I left Laramie thinking hard about why *Squamish* was not famed in song and story. Surely fascinating events had happened to the people who had settled and worked in and around that town. And even if such events had not happened, why could not Squamish be a locale for fictional occurrences, just as Laramie was, given that the towns were of similar size? I also pondered what a difference it must be to grow up in or near places that are considered worth celebrating in the culture around you.

"Culturally things are somewhat better for you," I told the class. "After all, Canadian literature is now taught in our colleges. And here and there in certain high schools like this, you students are shown writing about your own city and your own era, as we never were.

"Of course, there's still an enormous distance to go," I continued. "For example, you'll see lots of movies about teenagers attending high schools. But," I intoned, "these films won't be based on what it's like to go to *this* school. You'll see movies about Hollywood High, but nobody is making a movie about Van Tech Secondary."

At this comment the class broke into loud laughter. I stared at them, bewildered, until the teacher came to my rescue. A U.S. film crew had recently spent some days at Van Tech filming a movie, she explained. But, like many of the movies made in the past few years in B.C., the locale was supposed to be the U.S. In fact, the setting for the film shot in the halls and classrooms of Van Tech was supposed to be . . . Hollywood High.

These students were aware that part of their own reality was about to be presented to them transformed into somebody else's. And yet they also had a teacher willing to show them that their own streets and mountains, and the experiences of their parents and fellow citizens, could also be the subject of culture (in the poems they were considering that term). Unlike my introduction to culture, these students were at least conscious that different possibilities for culture do exist.

But if we start to consider in more detail that cultural possibility called "Canadian culture," to better understand what value it might have, the first problem surely is: *which* Canadians are we talking about? What is the range of experiences and ideas currently included in Canadian cultural artifacts? *Whose* Canada do we mean when we speak of "Canadian culture?"

We can see this problem illustrated by a trip, say, to the B.C. Provincial Museum. Visitors are shown, among other exhibits, the interior of a "typical Victorian-era house." But this display is false. On view is the interior of a home belonging to people *of a certain social class* — in this case, a fairly well-to-do family. We are not shown the interior of a "Victorian-era house" belonging to, for instance, a mine employee or a millworker. Then, as now, there was not one

British Columbia, but many existing simultaneously. If we are to assess the worth of Canadian culture, we had better start by being clear about the particular Canada a given cultural artifact speaks about or to.

I have noticed cultural producers or commentators sometimes attempt to avoid this task by explicitly or implicitly denying that economic divisions between Canadians exist. Or, if these divisions are observed, their cultural significance is denied. A fascinating attempt to simultaneously *recognize* these economic differences, while downplaying their *significance,* was made by Petro Canada in their television ads promoting the oil company's sponsorship of the 1988 Winter Olympics torch relay. In the ad the inhabitants of a small town are shown getting ready to watch the relay runners carry the torch through their community. We see a well-dressed business-man shutting up his shop, and we also see a welder turn off his torch and push his goggles up onto his forehead, in preparation to leave to witness this momentous event.

Seconds later we observe these representatives of the two major economic divisions of Canadian society — employers and employ-ees — stand side by side in a crowd watching with evident pride and joy the Olympic torch being carried past. The welder turns to the businessman and gives him a mild, comradely punch on the shoul-der, as evidence that the emotions surrounding this event have dissolved class distinctions and, by gosh, we Canadians are all in this together. The businessman wipes away a tiny tear from his eye. Of course, this sort of thing is crude propaganda, but it does arise out of an actual wish people have for unity, for a feeling of community. That wish may not be the motivation that inspires museum direc-tors, cultural commentators, and corporations to blur the distinc-tions between the lives of the majority of Canadians and the lives of the minority who have economic control over us. But it is certainly that wish that causes many Canadians to accept uncritically this view of their own society and culture.

In fact, not even colossally expensive public spectacles such as Calgary's 1988 Winter Olympics or Vancouver's Expo 86 can abolish the differences in economic interest between those who are employed for a living and those who employ others for a living. Large taxpayer-funded spectacles are inevitably the occasion for corporate advertisers and public relations experts to generate a great wave of sentimentality about a region or the nation in the hope of motivating sales of various products. But the reality remains that no businessperson would reverse a decision to fire somebody on the grounds that the person affected is an Olympic supporter, or because the man or woman to be fired is a fellow *Albertan* or *Canadian*. Nor would any employer refrain from automating or moving operations to a different part of the world in search of cheaper labour costs on the grounds of patriotism.

Corporations like Petro Canada may call themselves "proudly Canadian," but the same federal government that owns both Petro Canada and Canada Post did not hesitate for an instant to employ scabs in an attempt to break the strikes by Canadian postal workers in the summer of 1987. The issue at stake, as in most strikes, was the employer's wish to save money. On the other side of the dispute was employee resistance to measures that would worsen working conditions and result in a lower standard of living. The consequence of a victory for the employer's demands would be to depress the quality of life for one group of Canadians, surely a strange technique for demonstrating pride in one's country.

Always, then, we have to watch closely when people begin to invoke "Canada" to justify culture — or any other activity or cause. Who represents this "Canada" we are asked to identify with? And while sorting this question out, we have to be clear about a second matter: our own idea of what a *country* is. In other words, what is Canada *for*? Does it primarily exist to provide a place where men and women who own enterprises can maximize profits? Or is it intended to be a sort of cooperative venture, whereby all those who live here work jointly to ensure the maximum happiness for one another? When a federal government proposes to spend $8 billion to obtain a nuclear submarine fleet rather than, say, to provide food for the users of food banks in the country's cities and towns, that government acts on a specific belief in the purpose of Canada.

Or is it the nation's aim to provide a free and democratic

environment in which the people who live here can make their own decisions and solve their own problems? If so, how far should this democracy extend? Within the past seventy-five years we have seen political democracy spread to women and Orientals — two groups formerly denied the vote. But have we now attained a fully democratic society? Is it right that, as at present, democracy ceases for the majority of us the moment we enter the office door or the factory gate? If we are adult enough to decide the affairs of state in national elections, are we not adult enough to control democratically the enterprises where we work? How democratic is a situation where a handful of nonelected Canadians have enormous economic and social power over the rest of us during our hours each day at the job?

For me, thinking about the value of Canadian culture includes being definite about what group of Canadians are referred to, and whose vision of the country's purpose is being openly or indirectly endorsed. Yet the impassioned spokespersons on behalf of Canadian culture seldom stipulate which Canadians and what concept of Canada they mean. Instead, I hear three major arguments repeated when these spokespersons do try to indicate *why* Canadian culture might be worth protecting.

One explanation they give for culture's importance in Canadian society is that culture, especially high culture, raises us out of the humdrum of daily life, inspires us, gives us new vision. "Culture lifts us out of ourselves," as one speaker put it at an anticutback rally I attended in Edmonton in the 1970s.

However, the capacity to lift us out of ourselves is the characteristic of a narcotic. Any narcotic — whether alcohol or some other recreational drug — gives us the illusion of escape from the everyday, fills us with dreams of other possibilities for our lives, and then cruelly returns us to the same daily existence from which we sought to remove ourselves. Far from being a means of escape from our present situation, a narcotic reinforces present realities by keeping us occupied with illusions instead of letting us gain knowledge or skills to solve our personal and social problems. Any narcotic, like going to cultural events, is potentially addictive precisely because it does *not* lead to changes in our daily life. The only way we can feel that good again is to have another hit, to take another trip into a beautiful never-never land.

Mainstream ballet, for example, seems to me to teach that the essential truths of this world are to be found in fantasy, far away from the joys and difficulties of everyday existence. Like much of mainstream culture, ballet's celebrations of artificial and impossible characters and situations appears to offer me escape from the sources of my daily unhappinesses and problems. As we have seen, though, such escape is bogus, since nothing is altered in my daily life by this cultural product. I gain neither understanding about the causes of my difficulties nor ideas about overcoming injustices inflicted on myself or others. At the end of the performance I am returned to a world that is exactly as I left it. I may have gained a memory of some delightful moments, but I also know what I must purchase to experience those moments again.

And as for the Romantic concept that exposure to high culture will influence people's day-to-day behaviour for the better, World War II appears to have put an end to that notion. The image of Germany, once considered the most cultured nation in Europe, adopting Nazism as a means out of its difficulties demonstrates conclusively mainstream culture's narcotic rather than rehabilitative function. Consider the symphony orchestras the Germans organized from concentration camp inmates for the enjoyment of the camps' guards. How responsive to human feelings did experiencing this wonderful music make the guards?

So it seems to me culture's alleged ability to "lift us out of ourselves," or make us "better" people, is a bogus proposition. A second dubious attempt to explain the usefulness of Canadian culture I hear from time to time is that Canadian culture defines who we are. When the "we" is not specified here, this argument seems to me absurd. *I* certainly do not feel defined by Karen Kain's dancing, or Margaret Atwood's new novel, or Bryan Adams's new record, or some video artist showing her or his work to a group of fellow artists at a state-supported gallery. All these artistic productions may be dazzling, accomplished, innovative, or may be less successful artistically. But I personally do not know anybody who considers their lives, their identity, defined by such activity.

And in British Columbia, at least, the gap in attitudes between various sectors of the population has become so pronounced it would be difficult to imagine any encompassing "British Columbian" point of view that a cultural artifact could define. In 1986, for example, the government of the day, duly elected by a slim majority, reduced already inadequate provincial welfare payments to offset its growing deficit. Funds were then allotted to provide $5,000 worth of fireworks every night for the six months of Expo 86. The gulf in values is enormous between those British Columbians who believe a community has a duty to help its members who require assistance, and those British Columbians who believe the community's first duty is to use its financial resources to attract tourists (i.e., customers with money from elsewhere). I have yet to see cultural artifacts that incorporate both sets of values to the satisfaction of those who hold these divergent views. Who, then, is the "we" this culture supposedly defines?

The third defence of the worth of Canadian culture that gets articulated is a monetary one. In this argument culture has value and should be supported because government subsidies to the arts generate profits for business. Advocates of this line of reasoning have the figures to show that each symphony ticket sold results in extra consumer spending on restaurant meals, taxis, baby-sitters, drinks after the concert, and so on. Similarly the Canada Council programme of support for public readings by Canadian authors is regarded as a subsidy of the airlines, plus a boost in book sales to the benefit of printers, papermakers, publishing houses, and bookstores.

Where this argument seems faulty to me is that it tries to create the impression that people are attracted to become artists in order to benefit business. I do not believe this is true. People I know who have become writers, painters, musicians, et cetera, did not do so out of a philanthropic wish to aid the downtrodden business community. They became involved in producing cultural artifacts because they want to express some truth as they see it, or because they enjoy play with words or sounds or forms or colours, or because they find being involved with the arts enables them to feel and think and observe life in new and exciting ways. Their obsession with whatever cultural form or forms they adopt amounts to a rejection of the concept so beloved of business that the only means to measure value on this planet is the dollar.

In my experience the business community senses this fundamental clash of values between the cultural world and themselves. If the dollar is *not* the paramount means of assessing worth in our society, then somebody who has adopted this philosophy has made a hideous error in her or his life. Overall, that is one main message of culture. So I do not find it surprising that I have never seen anyone opposed to an appreciation of the arts who was won over on the grounds that culture is good for some businesses.

In contrast to the three standard justifications of the usefulness of Canadian culture, I have a different reason for regarding Canadian culture as important. I believe culture that is about a clearly defined group of Canadians, that celebrates and explores their lives, can help provide these people with a sense of self-confidence. Such cultural artifacts suggest to these women and men that their lives are worthy of being the subject of art, and thus that what happens to them is significant. On the other hand, a lack of this self-confidence tangibly harms these people, individually and as a group, and leads themselves and the rest of the human family to overlook their achievements and potential.

The group of people that I feel should be the central focus of Canadian culture is the majority of those who inhabit our portion of the globe — those of us who are employed for a living. Since the governing influence on our lives is the job we do (or our lack of employment), any cultural artifact intending to articulate our personal and social existences would have to take into account what happens while we are at work and the ways our employment affects our time off the job. Furthermore, since many aspects and most nuances of how our work shapes us are known only to an *insider* to our situation, it is up to *ourselves* to create the culture that reflects and illuminates our lives.

At present a strict taboo surrounds an accurate portrayal of work in Canadian culture. With few exceptions an insider's look at what it is like to go to work each day in contemporary society is missing. And this taboo harms people. For example, because work is not considered culturally important, school curricula largely ignore the history, present form, and possible future of daily employment. As a result, students frequently embark on years of training for a trade or profession with only the vaguest or glossiest notion of what a job is like and of how this employment affects the human beings who perform it. The absence in our culture of any accurate depiction of our work also leads to a profound sense of isolation. We are aware we have certain problems at the job, or problems that arise away from work because of our employment. But perhaps we are the only ones who feel this way? Left unsure and isolated, we are less likely to search for a collective answer to our difficulties, a collective means to improve our lives.

A further negative consequence of the taboo is a mystification of how products and services come to exist. One consequence of this mystification is that when we do not know much about one another's jobs, do not know much about how the goods and services we need or want are created, it becomes easier to believe negative reports about people who in reality are very much like ourselves. That is, we are willing to accept the received idea that postal workers are lazy, people on strike are greedy, et cetera. Yet the more we accurately understand one another's working lives, the more readily we can feel a kinship with them, and can practise solidarity with them when they run into difficulties.

The negative consequences of the present taboo begin to disappear if our cultural world recognizes the importance of the work we do: how that work determines our standard of living and the amount of time and energy we have off the job, plus the ways our employment influences our beliefs, friendships, where we live, and much more. As *Canadian* employees, we are doubly disadvantaged when the cultural artifacts around us present neither our working lives nor our geographic and historical experiences. And since an accurate consideration of the working lives of women and of people of colour has also been largely absent from mainstream culture, these individuals face a triple and/or quadruple disadvantage in looking to Canadian culture as a source of self-esteem.

To me, then, culture has value when it breaks the taboo and gives a majority of Canadians self-confidence. And I do not make such an assertion just because I think self-confidence is a nice quality for people to have. I believe self-confidence is the root of democracy. If I do not consider myself important, why would I think I have the right to participate in determining what happens to me and to my community? Self-confidence on the part of the majority is *necessary* for the maintenance and extension of democracy. Since I consider democracy to be the form of social organization that offers the best chance for creating a fair, equitable, and happy society, I regard a culture that promotes self-confidence as a *requirement* for the preservation and enhancement of human dignity.

A culture that diminishes or retards people's self-confidence, either through what it proposes or omits, I believe is a threat to democracy. When what we do and who we are are not considered culturally significant, when our contribution to society is hidden behind "big names" (for example, when a corporate executive is said to "make" the product our labour and imagination help create, or an architect is described as having "built" the building we worked on), then the worth of our lives is diminished compared to the value of comparatively few other people. It is only a step from this to thinking that a "name" person is more important than we are, and hence that his or her thoughts, activities, opinions, and so on are more worthy and should have more weight than our own. This last idea, of course, is counter to the very basis of democracy.

And if we do not consider our lives important, then it is unlikely we will do much to change our lives for the better. Most movements in history that lead to a deepening and broadening of democracy begin with a belief among the activists that they *deserve* the changes they are battling for. In short, people involved with achieving social change have self-confidence. The barons who confronted King John to obtain the Magna Carta, no less than the men and women who fought for and won the eight-hour day, no less than the women who successfully struggled for the right to vote, all had the self-confidence that led them to demand changes that were considered radical, unnatural, impossible to the established wisdom of their day. If Canadian employees are to achieve an extension of democracy to that part of our lives where we do not yet have the right to vote — the workplace — we will need the self-confidence that we *deserve* democracy in every aspect of our social existence. Similarly if Canada is to survive as a nation, Canadians will need the self-confidence that we *deserve* to be a separate country.

I look to Canadian culture to give us this self-confidence, but in a positive, enabling way. The self-confidence as provided by culture must not shade over into arrogance, into myths of unity or power that are harmful to ourselves or others in the long run. We have the U.S. example of the myth of the cowboy. This myth leads to the mentality of the man with the gun who is a law unto himself (in Laramie, among other places). As celebrated in culture, the cowboy myth can pave the way for U.S. armed intervention in Third World struggles. This myth, incidentally, also obscures the *reality* of the cowboy as an underpaid agricultural labourer whose protests against living and working conditions have included from time to time strikes and efforts to organize unions.

I recognize that self-confidence is not given or denied people only by cultural artifacts. Unemployment undermines men's and women's sense of individual worth. And self-assurance can be a result of feelings of competency that education provides. Yet where schools teach people they are failures, or when access to self-enhancing education is thwarted (for example, by government reductions in operating funds and student aid programmes), development of self-confidence in individuals is again blocked. A social climate of permanent high unemployment, and reduced access to positive educational experiences, threatens the emergence of a culture that reinforces the importance of the daily successes and defeats of the majority of us.

Even with such obstacles, and with all the qualifiers I see as necessary for Canadian culture to be of value, I remain convinced that the cultural artifacts produced by Canadians can rise to the challenge. I am heartened by the appearance here of the new poetry, fiction, and drama written by people about their own daily work — however overwhelmed this material still is by the bulk of our cultural products. Because all Canadians share the strange experience of being culturally invisible in their own land, Canadian artists have the ideal background to understand the importance of articulating the lives of the previously hidden majority. I do not think it is an accident that the new imaginative writing about work appears more often in anthologies of contemporary literature by Canadians — and by U.S. women and people of colour — than it does in anthologies of writing by mainstream (i.e., mostly white and male) U.S. authors.

I am therefore optimistic that Canadian culture will assist the majority of Canadians to find the self-confidence we require. I am aware, however, that the success of this project demands a serious change in the artistic and academic status quo, since up to the present an accurate depiction of the lives of the majority of us has not been a goal of Canada's artistic or academic tastemakers — mainstream or avant-garde. Indeed, over the long haul the resistance of these authorities to admit the concerns of most Canadians into our artistic agenda may pose a larger threat to the development of Canadian culture than either free trade or cutbacks in government sponsorship of the arts.

2 A HOUSE WITHOUT BOOKS: THE WRITER IN CANADIAN SOCIETY

An incident that best sums up for me what it means to be a writer in Canada occurred in the summer of 1986 when I was on holiday at the north end of Vancouver Island. I was taking the ferry from Port McNeill to Alert Bay to visit the Indian museum there. On the deck of the ferry, standing by my car, I fell into a conversation with another driver. He was a fisherman, maybe in his mid-fifties, headed over to Alert Bay to pick up a net. He mentioned that his home port was Pender Harbour, on the Sunshine Coast north of Sechelt. Now Pender Harbour is not a large place, and happens to be the home of my friend, publisher, and fellow poet Howard White. So I asked the fisherman if he knew Howie.

Howard White is somewhat of a legend in the B.C. literary world. By trade he is a heavy equipment operator, and still has the contract to manage the Pender Harbour dump. So besides spending most of his time at his computer pushing large amounts of words around, Howie spends several hours a week at the controls of his bulldozer pushing large amounts of garbage around. And in addition to running his vital and thriving publishing house, Harbour Publishing, Howie edits the highly successful magazine about the B.C. coast, *Raincoast Chronicles*. On the side, he is a well-received poet, and his oral history books routinely appear on the B.C. bestseller list.

But standing then on the deck of that ferry, I watched the eyes of the fisherman darken as I mentioned Howie's name. "Howie White?" the fisherman asked, recoiling from me. A certain tone entered his voice, the tone people reserve for talking about in-laws they despise, or child molesters. "Sure, I know him. Doesn't he *write?*"

This attitude of utter disdain expressed by the fisherman towards writing encapsulates for me the relationship of Canadian authors to their society. At best a Canadian writer is a marginal figure. But that marginality leads a majority of Canadians to view writers as people engaged in a socially unacceptable, if not perverse, activity.

Before I continue, though, let me quickly define my central terms. When I speak of a Canadian writer here, I mean writers of prose fiction, drama, or poetry. Also, when I speak of Canadian society, I refer here to mainstream English-language society. In my experience literary authors associated with ethnic minorities have a different relationship to readers within that minority than they do to English-speaking Canadians as a whole. For instance, Andrew Suknaski is a nationally recognized writer who has detailed in his poems the lives of Ukrainian settlers in rural Saskatchewan. Because of this effort, Suknaski's work has been received with enthusiasm by many members of the Ukrainian-Canadian community. But when Suknaski turns to address the general Canadian population, not as a representative of a minority but simply as a *poet,* he faces the same unease and scorn that greets the rest of Canada's literary practitioners.

Now since cultural values are transmitted by education, I believe a root cause of the marginal status accorded Canadian authors is our school system. One of the triumphs of public education in Canada is that we have been able to teach the overwhelming majority of people to read while simultaneously so turning them off reading that, once they are out of school, most never read a book again.

In my experience a majority of people who endure our high school or university English classes do not afterwards regard reading books — and especially literary titles — as a means of enhancing their lives. Those few who do continue to read mainly see literature as entertainment, fantasy, escape. I sometimes hear poetry mocked at as irrelevant because "hardly anyone reads poetry." As far as I can see, hardly anyone reads any kind of literature. In the course of my life I go into house after house where there are *no books*. In the homes of many of my friends, although most of them at least finished high school, there are *no books* — of any kind.

When I taught in the early 1980s at David Thompson University Centre in Nelson, B.C., we set a little quiz for students entering the writing programme in which, among other things, we asked if they could name three Canadian writers. Almost none could. And these were students who not only were interested enough in learning to seek postsecondary education, but were presumably interested enough in literature to enter a creative writing programme. More recently I have been teaching at community colleges in a Vancouver suburb and in B.C.'s Okanagan Valley. One of my assignments asks each of my students to give a presentation to their classmates on something they learned about how to write from their reading of a contemporary novel, book of short fiction, playscript, or collection of poems. I find the response depressing. "But I don't *read*" is one protest I hear *every* term when I announce this assignment. Most students eventually choose to discuss the work of authors such as the popular U.S. horror writer Stephen King. A student once came up to my desk clutching a newspaper clipping of a personal advice column by Ann Landers. "Is it okay if I do my presentation on this?" the student inquired.

I am convinced that by what we teach, we teach a system of values. If the majority of our population decides the reading of good literature is irrelevant to their lives, and looks with indifference or suspicion on those who produce literature, these are value judgements that Canadians have acquired through their schooling — since school is the *only* place most of us ever meet people whose job it is to try to show us the worth of literature.

When we examine most high school English curricula, it is not difficult to see why students might conclude literature is pointless, boring, or escapist. I worked some years ago in a suburban Vancouver high school as an English department marker. The students whose papers I marked were bothered by the usual issues facing adolescents — and the rest of us — today: sex, drugs, family breakup, the uncertainty of long-range occupational goals, immediate employment opportunities (in a province where the official unemployment rate has stood at ten percent for many years) and — if any work can be found — job conditions. The assigned novels for grade eleven in those days were *Lord of the Flies*, a science fiction tale about a group of English schoolboys marooned on a tropical island during World War III, and *A Separate Peace*, about some boys at a private boarding school in rural New England during World War II. If you set out to *design* a reading curriculum more removed from contemporary suburban Canadian high school students' lives, you would be hard-pressed to come up with better titles. Furthermore, these students would write in their essays over and over again — presumably echoing or mis-echoing what they were taught in class — how *Lord of the Flies* portrays a microcosm of human existence. I would patiently scrawl across their papers: "But there are no *women* in that book."

For it was the women's movement that showed us that if in our teaching of literature we omit an accurate account of the experiences of women, we teach that those experiences have no value. My own mission as a writer has been to add that if in our teaching of literature we omit an accurate account of the experiences of daily work, we teach that such experiences have no value. Generations of Canadians have grasped that when the literature we are taught omits the experiences of Canadians — as a people who share a history and geography, as well as individuals who must function in a society and work force organized in a particular way, then this literature teaches us our own experiences — past, present, and future — have no value.

English classes where this literature is taught thus obliterate who we are and what we have so painfully managed to accomplish and to discover about our world. It is no wonder a majority of us do not want to pursue reading any further, except for whatever escape from daily cares some reading offers. And no wonder we look with disbelief and contempt at anyone who actually wants to write *more* stuff that says we and our lives are worthless.

Let me hasten to acknowledge, however, that here and there in the educational system are English teachers who work very hard to right this great wrong. These marvellous women and men approach even the authorized curriculum with tremendous imagination and energy and often succeed in inspiring readers from among their students. Unfortunately, as house after house without books in Canada incontestably reveals, such teachers are definitely the exception. Every Monday during the school year, in educational institutions all across Canada, most students will be back learning that literature has nothing to do with them. Their only *possible* revenge is to have nothing to do with literature.

But the marginalization of Canadian writers is not solely due to the schools. Canada in its thirteen decades of existence has managed to transform itself from a colony of Britain into a colony of the United States. Since one of the hallmarks of every colony is a lack of self-confidence, even if we *were* a nation of readers, we would be mainly readers of British and American books.

I can still get a rueful laugh in high school classrooms I visit when I talk about how when I was a young student I thought poetry was something written by dead Englishmen. My sense is that the curriculum in poetry has not changed all that much. Many of my literature professors at the University of B.C. were live Englishmen, or Canadians who thought like Englishmen. I can still remember the comment of one when a fellow student raised a question to do with U.S. authors. "*American* literature?" the professor sneered. "Ah, yes. I really must sit down and read it some *afternoon.*" You can well imagine this professor's attitude towards *Canadian* literature.

And to demonstrate the present economic and cultural power of the behemoth we live beside, one anecdote should do. On the same holiday trip I referred to earlier, I was camped for a time on a beach on northern Vancouver Island's west coast at San Josef Bay. After about a week, we had to hike out for more food, and so headed for the nearest store at Holberg. Holberg, although nominally a village, is really a large logging camp, but the camp commissary serves as the grocery for the region.

Looking for something to read, I discovered in the Holberg commissary a wire rack of novels, such as is found in urban drugstores or supermarkets. Inserted into a holder on the top of the rack was a computer-generated printout listing the current week's bestsellers as compiled by the *New York Times.*

Such is the awesome might of U.S. industry that they can supply the Holberg commissary, many kilometres in the bush at the northern tip of Vancouver Island, with the list of what someone in New York City has determined *that same week* to be the latest bestsellers. In addition, most of these U.S. bestsellers were available in the commissary. I do not have to tell you that the list did not include any Canadian books, nor that a list of current B.C. or Canadian bestsellers was not posted at Holberg. I do not have to tell you that there were no Canadian books of any kind for sale in the Holberg commissary.

People are sometimes shocked by the economic consequences of this marginalization of the Canadian writer. Sales of Canadian literary titles are for the most part staggeringly low. A novel typically will sell about two thousand copies in hardback over a couple of years. If the novel sells for, say, $22.95 and the author gets the standard royalty of ten percent, the author earns about $4,600 from his or her creation — over two years. "But what about Margaret Atwood?" people sometimes object. "She gets six-figure advances." Okay. But according to a 1985 *Financial Post* survey, out of the dozens of novels by Canadians published in Canada each year, only *five* will reach sales of five thousand copies — the mark of a Canadian bestseller. Priced at $22.95, those five thousand copies will net each of those five, extremely rare, bestselling Canadian fiction authors the glorious sum of $11,500 before taxes. That $11,500 is not much for the amount of time, thought, and energy a novel takes to produce. And it certainly is not adequate to live on.

The numbers for poetry sales are of course worse. An ordinary Canadian book of poems will sell about four hundred copies a year. At a retail price of $8.95 that brings the author the grand total of $358 for her or his creativity, sweat, and tears.

In fairness I should mention that the determination and know-how that enables the U.S. book industry to service the Canadian hinterlands where the Canadian book industry apparently is unable to go does not mean the average American author is better off economically than a Canadian one. In 1981 *Publishers Weekly* reported on a survey of U.S. literary and nonliterary writers, which concluded that "figures for authors from households of varying size suggest that writing income places most authors below the poverty line." In fact, despite the articles on rich and famous writers in *People* magazine, *Publishers Weekly* reported only five percent of U.S. authors can support themselves from their writing. Part of the reason for such a low percentage is that although the U.S. population is ten times greater than the Canadian one, most books in the U.S. do not sell ten times better than their counterparts in Canada. For example, a book of poems in the U.S. usually sells about a thousand copies and can sell as few as the equivalent book in Canada. Also, most novels do not do much better in the U.S. than here. A 1980 survey of U.S. children's book authors who had been writing for twenty years or more found that half of them earned less than $1,000 a year from their writing, and two-thirds earned less than $5,000 a year from their writing.

As in Canada, writers in the U.S. have no safety net of income indemnity plans, extended health care programmes, or other job benefits. Concerning pensions, James Lincoln Collier, who wrote the 1981 *Publishers Weekly* article I mentioned, makes a ghoulish observation. He points out that a successful writer's best hope for retirement is to fall facedown over his or her keyboard from a heart attack while his or her markets are still holding up.

In the U.S., as here, most authors must support themselves by working at another job as well as writing. Like anyone in the work force who moonlights, authors who have two jobs often seriously damage their ability to relate meaningfully to other human beings — threatening both family and social life and negatively influencing the message of what these authors write. In Canada, as in the U.S., a network of public and private granting agencies provides some additional writing-related revenue for authors. But none of it, save an occasional grant providing subsistence income for up to twelve months, fundamentally alters the writers' economic status. In this country the Canada Council provides support for public readings by authors and organizes payment to writers for the use of their books by libraries. Yet both of these programmes have financial caps: readings are limited by the Council to seven a year, or $1,400 maximum annually, and the library use payment is capped at $4,325 a year. Very few authors receive the maximum in these programmes. Once again the economic marginalization of the Canadian writer is in no way changed by such government aid.

If things are so bleak for writers in Canada — sociologically, culturally, economically — why do any of us continue to write? I think each of us finds a satisfactory answer, or stops writing. For myself, I observe that although only a few people make a living and/or are considered culturally significant because they can dance, nevertheless millions of Canadians enjoy getting out on the dance floor. A similar observation can be made of people who, for example, fly kites or play guitar.

I believe writing, for at least this Canadian author, is no different than kite flying or guitar playing is for someone to whom kite flying or guitar playing has become a central part of his or her existence. In such circumstances building and flying kites represents more than a hobby, although not a livelihood, either. Rather, the challenges and sense of accomplishment that kite flying provides approach being an obsession. I have written elsewhere of why I am convinced what I have to say as a writer is important, even if no one is listening. I am fascinated, too, by the difficulty of trying to express myself in a manner that delights a reader while it acquaints that reader with information I believe is crucial. This is a task that seems unquestionably worth a lifetime of struggle, of small achievements and large defeats, even if this is a battle about which a majority of my fellow citizens could not care less.

3 MARTY AND ZIEROTH: TWO WRITERS FROM ELSEWHERE

I The Elsewhere

In his book on cosmogony, *A Brief History of Time,* Stephen Hawking discusses the concept of "elsewhere" as used in the study of space-time. An event can occur in our galaxy, such as the flaring out of a star. Yet because of the immense scale of the universe, information about this wonder may not reach a specific observer — on Earth, for instance — for a period of time. From the point of view of a hypothetical omniscient watcher of the cosmos, the star's death has indeed occurred. But although this information about the star is travelling towards the observer on Earth at the speed of light, the news of the star's destruction will not reach her or him for a very long time yet. In the interval the demise of the star — from the perspective of the observer on Earth — is said to have occurred in a region of space-time designated as the "elsewhere." "Elsewhere" lies outside our ordinary, familiar, observable reality. And yet occurrences have happened there that are *real,* and that one day will be brought to our attention.

I believe that when Canadian literature is critically assessed at present we are omitting excellent writers whose powerful, resonant, and highly crafted work exists now in the elsewhere. A majority of those who study our national literature mainly see, instead of these writers, a group of authors who are associated with a cultural event about which information *has* reached the place where the current observers are. This event is the supernova of a national fascination with Canadian literature that occurred in the late 1960s and early 1970s. So bright was this supernova that it illuminated many areas of Canadian life that before were largely uninterested in our historical and contemporary imaginative writing: academia, the news media, the entertainment media.

One could trace the appearance and disappearance of this dazzle of attention to our literary practitioners by scanning the table of contents of, say, *Saturday Night* magazine under Robert Fulford's editorship. Here, early during the period in question, is found an increasing coverage of Canadian books and authors, plus the inclusion of samples of these writers' latest productions. This coverage rises to a peak and then fades, almost disappearing when replaced by a belief that the business world, rather than literature, is the significant source for understanding and articulating our country.

The vanishing of an interest in serious contemporary Canadian writing among nonspecialists has had a number of effects on our literature since the supernova. As any performer (or teacher) knows, the audience has a decided influence on the quality of a performance. An attentive, responsive audience calls forth the best in a performer. If the identical material is presented to an indifferent or less demonstrative audience, however, the performance will often seem less successful both to the performer and individual audience member. So the waning of a wider public concern with Canadian writing and writers has led, predictably, to a certain lack of self-confidence in many of our authors.

This situation gets expressed in a number of ways, including a less supportive literary environment. That is, writers are harsher with one another in reviews, criticisms, within literary organizations, and so on. The missing confidence in themselves as artists is sought by means of attacks on other writers. Even a casual glance at the harangues published in the internal bulletin of the Writers' Union of Canada reveals attitudes far distant from those of the participants in the supernova who helped found the group. Another development that might have been anticipated as a response to a shrinking public interest is the proliferation of writing that is addressed to a specific circle of specially trained authors and readers: writing that requires familiarity with a number of specialist critical texts before it can be comprehensible to a general reader.

But the burning out during the 1970s of the blaze of increased attention paid to Canadian literature has also affected the academic appreciation and study of our imaginative writing. For the most part, as mentioned above, the news about Canadian literature on which the telescopes (and microscopes) of our academicians and teachers has remained tightly focused concerns those contemporary and historical authors prominent during the supernova. These writers have continued to receive the overwhelming bulk of attention during the decades since the stellar explosion swelled and guttered. This attention includes not only papers and dissertations, but also appearances in teaching anthologies and curricula, and thus designation as the established canon of Major Canadian Literature. News of much superb writing created by authors not prominent during the supernova has simply not reached our scholars and their students yet.

The theory behind the selection of certain works of literature as worthy of study (and hence subsequently worthy to be taught in our schools and universities and, ideally, incorporated into the daily lives and consciousnesses of our citizens) is that the chosen literature has been judged to be the best writing produced in a given era. Much has happened in the late twentieth century, however, to call into question *who* does this judging, and what biases (hidden or overt) influence the awarding of the label "best" to certain artistic works.

The English art critic John Berger has shown how the social milieu in which a given work of art is produced enormously influences how the work will be received by the first group of responders to that art (critics, patrons, et cetera), and hence by the general public who look to these people as experts in evaluating artistic worth. The values that this art endorses or rejects — either in that art's form or content — are assessed and compared to the values held by the power structure of the contemporary society. Berger argues in *Ways of Seeing,* for instance, that landscape painting first became validated by English society when landholders began to acquire the surplus cash and education to want artistically rendered representations of their property (or of real estate they admired and/or conceivably could later possess). In our own time we have heard men and women associated with the labour movement, with the women's movement, and with the struggles for social justice of native people and people of colour suggest that the experts who usually get to award the tag "best" to artistic productions have personal cultural biases that render the term highly suspect. Furthermore, the effect of these biases is an artistic canon skewed away from any reasonable representation of Canadian life and thought.

I believe the increased interest in Canadian literature that produced the supernova was sparked by a specific historical moment in Canadian society: a period when within our national power structure those men and women whose financial interests favoured an independent Canada were on the ascendant. I think these business people were often associated with industries or services that benefited from an independent national existence, a separate national identity. Hence they looked around for what distinguishes the inhabitants of this country from others who share this continent and planet. They found in our literature, among the other arts, a portrayal of environments, attitudes, characters, situations, and values that seemed to them to suggest some differences, some uniquenesses, that could justify our collection of communities and networks of trade and transportation calling itself a nation.

From my reading of history, however, I observe there has always been a tension among Canadian business leaders between a posture of independence ("no truck or trade with the Yankees") and a posture of unqualified acceptance of the reality that our biggest market and biggest supplier of manufactured goods is the country to the south . . . a country in which many Canadians have friends and relatives, and in which many of us retire, vacation, shop. At present the latter group of businesspersons seem decidedly to possess the greatest influence in our national life. These owners of, and/or believers in, large a-national corporations appear to owe allegiance strictly to the bottom line. There are no benefits, as they see it, in supporting a specific nation through tax money or rote lip service to patriotism. Why tolerate a proliferation of countries when business, and hence profit, is enhanced by the fewest possible local restrictions? As these ideas have gained more and more adherents, we have entered a period of common markets, runaway shops, special economic zones, and free trade. To such businessmen and women most national groupings seem anachronistic at best, impediments to profit at worst. And as the representatives of these ideas gained ascendancy in Canada, it became clear they regard art that speaks of human existence in a specific region or social class or era as either worthless or dangerous. From their viewpoint artistic productions, like all human artifacts, are commodities (actual or potential) rather than, say, sources of information or of a critical outlook or of an exploration of emotions. Art thus ideally should be as mute as any commodity — a load of lumber, a running shoe. Meanwhile our media, taking their cues from the money people, have duly shifted attention away from the arts as a central means of defining our existence. And so currently the arts, including literature, have resumed the traditional marginal position they have held in Canadian society since pioneer days.

Yet the brief supernova of wider interest in our literature set in motion a number of corollary events, including the increased establishment of programmes in Canadian literature in our postsecondary institutions. Hence we have witnessed the graduation of a new corps of experts in this field (whose students, given the standard operating procedures of our English departments, are in turn transformed into teachers and scholars of this subject area). The stellar light dimmed, but the observatories and research stations created to study the phenomenon are in place, staffed, and hard at work.

I am convinced, however, that there is much fine Canadian writing currently in the elsewhere. I want to focus here on two authors whose first books (in 1973) fall within the last fiery pulses of the stellar explosion. These writers, Sid Marty (born 1944) and Dale Zieroth (born 1946), seem to me apt representatives of the artistic accomplishments and delights that lie unobserved within the elsewhere. As well, Marty and Zieroth are among the foremost — both chronologically and artistically — to be concealed in the post-supernova elsewhere. Their works are outstanding examples of an enormous talent, able to amaze and inspire and give pleasure to a wide range of Canadian and other readers should the news of these writers' existence ever reach the gatekeepers of our literature and pass through.

I feel the critical and academic neglect of Marty and Zieroth, specifically, is mainly due to their appearance in the waning days of the supernova, too late for information about the high quality of their writing, of their contribution to Canadian literature, to have yet registered in the instruments of the nation's literary observatories. No other explanation for the neglect makes sense to me. At its best the quality of their writing is at least as fine by any demonstrable measure as that of the canonical Earle Birney, Leonard Cohen, Irving Layton, Dorothy Livesay, Eli Mandel, P. K. Page, Al Purdy, Raymond Souster. As presences in the world of Canadian letters, each has achieved as much or more as had Margaret Atwood, Dennis Lee, and Michael Ondaatje when they were first recognized as worthy of ongoing critical attention. To those who argue a Toronto bias permeates critical reception of Canadian imaginative writing, I would point out that both Marty's and Zieroth's books have been mainly issued by major Toronto literary publishers (McClelland and Stewart in Marty's case; House of Anansi, now owned by Stoddart, for Zieroth).

Marty's collections of poems — *Headwaters* (1973) and *Nobody Danced with Miss Rodeo* (1981) — describe and illuminate a life lived in the Rocky Mountains, no less accepted as a symbol of Canada than the south-central region of Ontario. His autobiographical account of his years as a park warden in the mountain national parks, *Men for the Mountains* (1978), has been continuously in print since publication, not only in Canada but with U.S. publishers (the Sierra Club, The Mountaineers). *Men for the Mountains* has also been published in Germany and Japan. Marty enjoys considerable attention in western Canada as a writer and speaker on environmental subjects and was commissioned by Parks Canada to write the official history of the mountain parks, *A Grand and Fabulous Notion* (1984).

He is also an accomplished folksinger whose recent cassette, *Let the River Run* (1990), offers subtle and stirring lyrics merging the author's deep commitment to wilderness, rural, and domestic life.

Zieroth's collections of poems are *Clearing* (1973), *Mid-River* (1981), *When the Stones Fly Up* (1985), and *The Weight of My Raggedy Skin* (1991). Zieroth's finely polished poems have depicted his growing up on a Manitoba farm in a German immigrant community, and his subsequent life in the Rocky Mountain village of Invermere, B.C., and then on the B.C. coast. More recently much of Zieroth's writing has centred on contemporary family life, especially fatherhood. His poems, on any topic, appear consistently in the major Canadian literary magazines, including *The Malahat Review, Poetry Canada Review,* and *Canadian Literature.* For many years he has been the editor of *Event,* itself one of the country's most important literary magazines and he teaches in the writing programme at Douglas College in New Westminster, B.C.

Yet almost no critical articles have appeared on either Marty or Zieroth. For instance, a survey of the *Canadian Periodical Index* for 1989 shows nothing written about Marty or Zieroth. By comparison five articles about Atwood and three about Ondaatje were indexed that year. Neither Marty nor Zieroth have individual entries in the latest edition of Mel Hurtig's *The Canadian Encyclopedia.* Neither appear in such widely adopted teaching anthologies as Daymond and Monkman's *Literature in Canada* (Gage, 1978) or Weaver and Toye's *Oxford Anthology of Canadian Literature* (1981) or Bennett and Brown's *An Anthology of Canadian Literature in English* (Oxford, 1983). Marty appears in neither Atwood's *New Oxford Book of Canadian Verse* (1982) nor Lee's *New Canadian Poets 1970-85,* even though the latter was issued by Marty's Canadian publisher.

Brief descriptions follow of some of what I find admirable in Marty's and Zieroth's work. I hope by this means to demonstrate that these writers — among others — are indeed treasures of the elsewhere, and greatly deserve (and handsomely repay) the sort of critical attention currently focused on those other excellent authors who had the good luck to be part of the supernova. Since interest in the environment has become ever more fashionable (and popular with students), it is worth noting that both Marty and Zieroth have written extensively and movingly over the years about the landscape and wilderness, and the place of themselves and our species within it. And both have based their responses to the natural world on their insider's experience of years of living and working in the wilderness. Both authors have also written effectively about fatherhood and about the family. The women's movement has justly pointed out the lack in the literary canon of male involvement in parenting. Yet out in the elsewhere both Marty and Zieroth have tender and striking poems on this topic.

I should add that neither Marty nor Zieroth necessarily agrees with how I depict their situation. Indeed, in conversation with Zieroth he has suggested that perhaps the problem lies in "nowhere" rather than "elsewhere." He points out that one consequence of the dominant corporate worldview has been the construction across Canada, as well as the rest of North America and many other places in the world, of malls and housing and office towers and daily lives that are entirely unrelated to the specific geographic locale in which these exist. To be among them is to be anywhere, that is, nowhere in particular. Even in nonurban settings tourist destinations supply nearly identical accommodation and services to their guests, regardless of which unique scenery or human-created marvel has supposedly drawn the tourists to this or that resort or hotel. As has been noted, it is now possible to go all around the world and stay in virtually the same room every night.

If this is the prevailing environment in which a majority of the population exists, it probably follows that a preference would be generated for art that is unspecific as to place, concentrating instead on the constituents of the art itself (forms, language, et cetera), or on magical or other nongeographic experiences. Writers like Marty and Zieroth, whose writing is planted firmly in identifiable locales, will perhaps seem out of step with, or even in opposition to, such present trends. Their writing quietly but convincingly asserts the value of unique locations, individuals, environments: it is definitely about a "where." Seen in its largest perspective, Marty's and Zieroth's "where" is the actual location of the inhabitants of this planet, as opposed to the fantasy life and backdrop continually seeking to envelop us through advertising, mass media, mass entertainment, and other messages from the corporate boardroom. As such, whether or not Marty's and Zieroth's art remains in the elsewhere, their writing affirms our real existence, and thus enriches — and challenges — us all.

II Sid Marty

Marty's *Men for the Mountains* opens with a supernatural event used to dramatize effectively one important theme of this nonfiction opus: that the history of the warden service is an important means by which to assess current attitudes towards the wilderness on the part of governments, parks employees, and the public. Here, then, is magic used not in an attempt to offer an escape from reality, but rather to dramatically enhance our understanding of it. *Men for the Mountains* begins and closes with an eerie encounter between the narrator and the ghosts of three of the parks' near-legendary former wardens.

Marty's mastery of descriptive detail — employed by him to make tangible both the natural world and these ghostly episodes — is revealed in his portrayal of the mountain cabin where the book starts. He presents the reader with references to the full array of senses. He makes sure we are aware of temperature: "I pulled the sleeping bag closer around my neck. It was the right place to be on a cold night." And also sound:

> I heard the reassuring cling of the bell on Cathy, my white mare. Through my two windows I could see the silver outline of mountains leaning over the cabin. A log crackled in the heater; my world was in order.

The arrival of the ghosts is heralded by descriptions familiar to readers of suspense yarns or watchers of horror films. The wind blows the door "open with a bang." When the voice of one of the spirits first speaks, we are shown Marty's fright: "My hair stood up and I spun around to stare into the dimly-lit room." This strategy is standard in horror movies. The sight of someone who is afraid is always more terrifying to an audience than the sight of what frightens that person. Our imaginations respond most strongly to other people's fear; what we imagine is more horrifying than anything Hollywood can come up with. And, in Marty's account, the ghosts make the traditional request that strong light not be shone on them. They are creatures of the dark, or of half-lit places. One of them cautions Marty when they first appear: "'Just leave that contraption alone. No sense in wasting fuel,' he added, stopping me in the act of reaching for the Coleman lantern." And, like the ghosts in many a fairy tale, Marty's spectral wardens feel the constraints of time. A ghost must return to the underworld before dawn. When the wardens become distracted for a moment over some comic business of offering Marty a drink of their awful liquor, "The wind moaned in answer outside, and the three stirred uneasily. 'Better get on with it, George,' Neish said."

At the close of the book, when Marty meets the ghosts for the second and last time, once more various physical senses besides sight are provided to make the unreal seem actual. As Marty opens the warden cabin door in the darkness, he smells "the odour of buckskin and wet wool." He feels "the heat on my face melting the ice out of my moustache," and when he drinks from a bottle of rum, he responds to "the sweet, slow burn of the spirits after hard work in the bite of a mountain night."

The effect of this careful effort to make the appearance of the former wardens in the book as real as possible is, in my view, twofold. First, the episodes demonstrate the power of strong writing — personally, no matter how many times I have reread these passages, I still get a prickling up the back of my neck when the narrator first comes face-to-face with the ghosts. Second, after the unsettling introduction of the former wardens in the first chapter, a reader of

Men for the Mountains never forgets that Marty's personal adventures in the warden service take place in a historical context. By extension a reader realizes that wherever she or he places herself or himself on the spectrum of attitudes towards the wilderness — from believing that the wilderness should be preserved untouched by humanity to regarding the wilderness as a potential source of wealth to be developed — there are historical precedents and events that consciously or unconsciously shape our views. This historical perspective applies as well to Marty's job. The work of a warden, like every contemporary job, has a history. Each aspect of a social task — hours of work, conditions, tools, wage structure — is the product of the men and women who came before us in the trade or similar trades. Any work autobiography that omits this awareness suffers from what the spectre of warden George Busby complains to the narrator about during the ghosts' first appearance: "Seems to me this here book of yours has 'eye' trouble. I done this and I done that — what about the rest of us? We figger we should be in there too somewhere." And, in fact, through these and other scenes Marty deftly weaves into his account of a contemporary warden's working life a very great deal of historical material, always as a means to explain and evaluate the present.

Marty's command of multisensual description also causes his portrayal of his *job* to seem more real to a reader. For example, at the start of chapter six ("Mustahyah") Marty does not merely tell the reader that one particular day in the Tonquin Valley he and his wife wake to discover fresh snow and bear tracks around the warden cabin. Instead, the narrator takes time to describe the varied effects of the snowfall, including "a veil of thin icicles that hung from the eaves above the windows." He even depicts the sight and sound of one specific bird: "Outside, a raven, perched on top of a gaunt, dead tree, greeted me with the musical throb of song those buzzards are capable of in their happier moments."

Here the descriptive technique serves to focus a reader's attention on the natural environment in which Marty's work is carried out. We never become so overwhelmed by the narrative about what happens to Marty, or other humans, that we lose awareness of the significance of the other characters in the story: the wildlife, plants, and terrain — all of which are affected by changes in weather and season as well as by the activities of people. We thus gain perspective on Marty's job. His story is important, but these detailed descriptions of what the plants, animals, and landscape are doing or look like continually emphasize that human beings are only one component in the natural order.

Of course, it is unlikely that when Marty sat down to write his work autobiography he recalled how on a certain morning in the Tonquin Valley there was a specific raven on a dead tree that gave a call. At the end of the book Marty tells the ghostly wardens that what he has learned by composing *Men for the Mountains* is that: "To tell the whole truth you have to write fiction." At the start of chapter six, the author's intent is to describe bird life as one part of the mountain landscape altered by the fresh snowfall, the arrival of winter. So Marty describes what *could* have been present in that scene, based on his personal experiences of such moments. Depictions like this one may not be literally true, but the effect of these sensuously rich descriptions gives a reader the *essential* truth of what Marty intends to portray.

Such fictionalizing for the sake of expressing "the whole truth" extends as well to how Marty organizes material in *Men for the Mountains*. For example, in chapter eight ("The Highway Blues") he aims to relate in one chapter the various aspects of a warden's employment when based in Banff townsite, rather than when posted to a remote wilderness area. Many incidents in this chapter (for example, warden Rick Kunelius explaining that he hangs his arm out an office window to "maintain contact with the alpine environment") may not have happened on the particular "3:00 p.m. to midnight shift" depicted in this chapter. The author instead is probably providing a *composite*, and hence not strictly true, work shift to give the reader a picture of the range of problems and their solutions a warden could reasonably encounter during one nine-hour shift in Banff. So some dramatic incidents — shooting an injured bighorn ram, fighting with some young drunks under the Bow Bridge — are included, along with a more humorous event:

Spalding, the golf ball-stealing coyote, attacking a golfer. If Marty had not adopted this strategy of picking representative incidents and depicting them as occurring in one shift, he would not have been able to show a reader all that such a shift could contain. Instead, Marty undoubtedly would have ended up *telling* how busy such a shift can be — a far less absorbing experience for a reader than the effect *Men for the Mountains* provides of following the narrator around from one fascinating difficulty to another within the framework of a nine-hour period.

In the incident involving the ram, Marty describes seeing on a bulletin board a news photo of a child feeding a bighorn ram. Marty says the photo is "glamourizing the feeding of animals, undermining all the work we were doing to discourage the practice." Later in the chapter, probably to illustrate why such feeding is dangerous for the animals since it teaches wildlife to hang around the highway, Marty describes how he tracks and must shoot a ram crippled by a speeding car. He recognizes the animal from the photo:

> I saw the massive horns, outlined against the right edge of the stream. There were at least seven annuli on them and one horn, the left one, was broomed off near the tip. It was the ram of the photograph, the ram that had fed from a child's hand.

It is *possible* that Marty did, during a shift, have to kill a ram featured in a "cute" news photo. But it is also possible that he shot a similar ram, or other animal, attracted to the highway through human thoughtlessness. The shooting could also have occurred on a different shift than the one when Marty first sees the animal's photo tacked up on a bulletin board. If Marty has changed actual events, making them more dramatic in this way (and it *is* quite a coincidence to encounter the exact same ram), he has done such fictionalizing for the purpose of underlining the folly of encouraging people to feed wild creatures, and about the repulsion a warden feels at having "to kill the very animals you are hired to protect." In the flow of *Men for the Mountains,* due to Marty's consummate skill at providing descriptive detail, it is easy to suspend disbelief from time to time for the purpose of being enjoyably taught some truth about the uses of the wilderness.

Marty's sure hand at selecting and rearranging material becomes evident, too, in comparing how incidents that appear in *Men for the Mountains* are also examined in his poems. In *Headwaters,* Marty's first book of poems (published five years before his work autobiography), "Shawn" covers some of the same events developed in chapter two of *Men for the Mountains* ("Euclid Never Threw the Diamond"). The setting of the poem and the most exciting event in the chapter are identical: in the words of the poem, "packing the trail crew's food and tents / down from Twin Falls in the rain" during a nighttime mountain lightning storm. The poem, though, restricts its focus to the narrator's attitude towards Shawn, the "old horse / furiously willing yourself to die." He praises the horse for "saving my skin" on the terrifying

> black, two foot wide trail
> switchbacking down the sidehills,
> the two mares biting your flanks
> to push us to death or home

Given that the poem is much shorter than the prose version, naturally a lot of detail has to be omitted in the poem. Some *central* aspects of the incident are missing in the poem, however; warden Bernie Engstrom disappears entirely, so the ride down the mountain in the night is described as involving only the speaker in the poem and horses. The sheer horror of the narrator's predicament is also not developed as fully as in the prose version:

> A bolt of lightning tore through the night in a brilliant flare that made the horses crowd together. At the shattering roar of the thunder, which followed immediately, they lunged back hard on the halters, pulling my arm back in one fierce twist of pain. The bolt was close enough to make my head spin, with the same jolt one gets from jumping off a four-foot-high fence and landing stiff-legged on the soles of the feet. An ozone and

> brimstone smell drifted up from the strike that had hit below us, which shattered the rocks like a shellburst. . . . I didn't want any more illumination after that brief glimpse of a mountain dropping away from under my left stirrup. The light had gleamed down the wet-streaked walls of rock to the water below in a terrible, beckoning vertigo that made my feet tighten convulsively in the stirrups.
>
> A mountain horse always walks on the outside of the tread, to keep itself clear of obstacles on the bank that might catch in its rigging, and it does this even on the steepest mountainside, walking on the very edge of the drop, like a confident aerialist on a wire hung in space. Occasionally a loose stone could be heard above the rush of the wind, clattering in a flurry of sparks down the cliff banks.

Also absent from the poem is Marty's near tumble over the mountain's edge when he slips off a wet log at the edge of the trail.

On the other hand, the danger to the narrator when he has to cut the mare June's halter rope, wrapped around her back legs, is not mentioned in the prose version — although the poem refers to "me with a jacknife sliding / among flying hooves." And at the end of the poem Shawn rears up when he and the narrator finally arrive at the trail crew's camp. Apparently startled by "the lantern's flame," the horse cuts his mouth on the bit as he attempts to flee from the light. The speaker in the poem says the crew "grieves" at the horse's reaction after such a valiant effort carrying their belongings down the dangerous trail through the storm and darkness. None of this — the attempt of the horse to pull back into the dark, injuring itself, and the crew's sympathetic response to the horse's pain — is found in the prose version.

Overall, the effect of Marty's choice of detail is to create both a tensely dramatic episode in his prose account, and a powerful poem that centres attention on the horse's life. By the end of the poem the horse is referred to as "the old man." After its heroic exertion on the perilous mountain trail, it tears off "with bloody lips /

furiously retreating into night." Here, as in many of Marty's poems, the literal and metaphorical blend together. The aged horse, already described as "furiously willing yourself to die," is at this point in its existence clearly raging towards death, as well as towards the literal darkness beyond the glow of the camp lights. Echoes of Dylan Thomas's "Do Not Go Gentle into That Good Night" hover subtly over the close of the poem, especially the speaker in that poem's wish for "old age" to "rage, rage against the dying of the light."

Two other examples of an overlapping of material in *Men for the Mountains* and *Headwaters* are the search for the drowned man in chapter three ("The Trap"), also portrayed in the poem "Drowning," and the forest fire-fighting episodes in chapter four ("Something's Burning") that are depicted as well in the poem "The Chaba Fire." As with the poem "Shawn" and the descriptions in chapter two, however, each version of these occurrences highlights different facets. Neither the prose nor the poem tells the *entire* story, nor gives the only possible interpretation of the *significance* of these events to the narrator. I believe it is a worthy feat to consider in two different genres the same material, and to have each treatment be fresh and novel. Everything Marty writes shows his keen and accurate eye for detail, detail that often only an insider to the experiences he presents could know. But Marty, as well, is in full command of what he wants to do with the raw data of events and locales — he can impressively ring the changes in two different genres, each fascinating to read.

Besides depicting the danger and beauty of outdoor life and work, Marty utilizes humour not only in *Men for the Mountains,* but also in his two books of poems. In "Packing Dynamite" in *Headwaters,* for instance, he relates how he is advised when packing horses "to keep your dynamite / and your blasting caps / in two separate places." But as his horses on the trail "battled for the lead," the containers for each get bashed together. The narrator in the poem comically describes his fear:

> My sun tan flaked off
> and I was a white and shining angel

> ready to take wing
> all in white pieces
> of a horse shit bomb

In "Too Hot to Sleep," from the same volume, the narrator and "my friend Birnie" doze off, perhaps while doing trail repair work on "a hot june morning / above Wapta Lake, the Kicking Horse Pass." A bear shows up and proceeds to investigate the sleeping Birnie. The animal "sniffed at Birnie's collar / at his ear, which he licked tentatively / causing Birnie to moan softly." After a conversation between the bear and the nervous narrator, the bear sniffs "at Birnie's armpit," snorts,

> and turned away, clattered down the creek
> popping his teeth, his hackles up
> Went out of sight
> around the shoulder of Mount Hector
>
> as Birnie woke up rubbing his eyes
> "Too hot to sleep" he said. Yeah.

In the above poem, among others, Marty uses some idiosyncratic punctuation, as many contemporary poets do, to keep the reader from simply reading the piece as prose. Here, statements uttered by the bear, or that take place in the mind of the narrator, are not set off by quotation marks. This serves to distinguish what gets said orally from what is a mental conversation between the bear and the narrator.

> "We were just going bear," I said quietly
> edging backwards
>
> Don't move too quickly will you, said Bear
> when you move, or better still
> don't move at all

Similarly the poet's omission of the comma between "going" and "bear" in the first line of this quotation serves a poetic purpose. Here the absence of the comma helps emphasize the rapid, frightened speech of the narrator when suddenly confronted by the bear.

The humour in "Too Hot to Sleep" arises from the tension of a potentially dangerous encounter between humans and wildlife, contrasted with a mundane supposed conversation between the bear and the narrator. This humour is enhanced by the irony of the sleeping Birnie, who is in the greatest peril, since he is unconscious of his plight. In "To a Black Bear," again from *Headwaters,* the humour once more arises from how Marty depicts an unexpected bear-human encounter, and from irony (including, in this case, a mutual retreat by the representatives of the two species).

Part of the humour in "To a Black Bear" also originates from a tradition of attributing human emotional responses to animals. The speaker in the poem says the bear shows up at "this sleepy warden station" because "it was a boring day / you wanted some fun." Of course the bear really shows up looking for food. Similarly the speaker says the bear "clawed some paint off the door" of the kitchen of "the boss's wife" in order "to hear her howl." This statement is hardly the reason why the bear attempts to enter the kitchen. The bear also is variously described as feigning indifference, "petulant," "sulking," and "embarrassed" — all human emotions or activities that combine to enhance the humour. The irony Marty employs includes ironic understatement at the moment when the narrator unexpectedly meets the bear in his own kitchen, where the narrator has gone to get bait for a culvert trap: "'Woof' you said / startled while trying the fridge / I forget what I said."

Marty's usual careful attention to details here helps convince us of the truth of what he relates. For instance, we are told precisely what the culvert trap is baited with. Exact details also heighten the moment of horrifying humour when the speaker and the bear suddenly confront each other: "Your black fur made quite a contrast / against that white porcelain." By providing such detail, the author also slows down the exciting events (since it takes longer to tell what is occurring). Even the mutual retreat is enhanced by detail ("I slipped and fell, / your claws lost traction"). This same technique is used in movies when action is shown in slow motion at intense moments so that these occurrences will seem to take longer, and hence allow the audience to savour the event and its importance.

Marty's poetic craft is also displayed in this poem through his variation of stanza lengths. For example, the most important instant in the poem, "We met in the kitchen," is presented as a stanza by itself. The white space before and after this line thus gives the reader extra time to ponder the significance of the encounter and antici-pate its consequences. Throughout the poem Marty shifts to a new stanza whenever the action takes a new turn. This *action, pause* (white space), *action* results in a sense of move and countermove on the part of the wayward bear and its human pursuer.

Humour is present, too, in various poems from Marty's second collection, *Nobody Danced with Miss Rodeo*. In the poem "I'm So Lonesome in the Saddle since My Horse Died," Marty creates a narrator who is himself a character relating an account of an Albertan "rangy-tang." Marty portrays this character-narrator not only by setting the whole poem in quotation marks, but also by capturing the colloquial speech of the poem's speaker:

> I disremember when it was
> he bought this mighty gelding, Boots.
> That pony really threw the honkytonk
> on Jim, he could not stay aboard.

The speaker in the poem tells of the various misadventures of a compatriot. The humour partially arises from the language used to relate the stories, and partially from the outrageous and often self-destructive behaviour of the poem's main subject. And yet the narrator is not without compassion for his acquaintance. The speaker mentions how the main character will refuse to wear gloves during roundup in order to be true to what he believes is the spirit of the old West. The narrator points out to him that the old-time cowboys probably could not afford gloves, but his friend refuses to listen to such advice: "Then he'd tag some old bitch of a Hereford, / and he'd burn them hands, Lordy! / Make yuh cringe to see it. . . ." The narrator recognizes that his subject is "a big stubborn kid" who "[gets] it wrong all the time." Nevertheless, the speaker ends by paying his subject the ultimate compliment: "Anyway, he was sure enough / aw-thentic cowboy. / He was a hand."

The final section of *Nobody Danced with Miss Rodeo*, "The Knife of Love," gathers together many of Marty's poems on family and fatherhood. Earlier in this volume the narrator of the poem "In the Arms of the Family" talks of the dangers of his mountain occupation: "The tools of the territory include / climbing ropes and helicopters / guns and dynamite." The narrator admits that "danger was my fix," and yet acknowledges that it is his family, "my woman and son," who can restore him to the "human moment":

> But he who was lost
> will wake up found, and right
>
> In the arms of the family
> that binds him again, to his life

The poems of "The Knife of Love" explore a number of dimensions of such life "in the arms of the family." "The Colours" is a moving look at varieties of premature death — a young climber drowned in a mountain creek, whose body the narrator helps pull out of the water, and the loss through miscarriage of the narrator's and his wife's baby. The poem juxtaposes colours associated with the drowned climber ("On the gravel bar / his shirt was scarlet / his limbs dead white") and the colours associated with the lost fetus (the "blue wells" of the wife's eyes, her "faded" garden roses, "and the bright clothes / unused in her nursery"). Relief comes with "the healing snow" of winter: "She and I / we'd had quite enough / of the flowers."

But Marty's sense of humour extends to family life, too. In "There Just Ain't No Respect" the narrator describes a disagreement between himself and his wife over the responsibility to move a vacuum cleaner left in a hallway. In the night the narrator gets up to stretch a leg, broken on the job, and his wife "sleepily" requests that he "check the kids' blankets." On the way to do so he stumbles over the vacuum cleaner and cuts his toe so that

> I'm tracking blood on the cold floor
> but I don't cry out, being
> a hardened husband
> Just
> cover the babies
> my teeth clenched
> and limp back to bed

Marty employs humour for poignant effect, as well. In "Revelation," quoted here in its entirety, he presents what for me is the funniest, most succinct glimpse possible of the uselessness of males in connection with some facets of child-rearing:

> I held our new baby
> against my bare chest
> and his four-day-old mouth
> explored my tingling skin
>
> Until he found a nipple
> my milkless, small
> and hairy nipple
>
> He battened on
>
> It was a major disappointment
> for both of us

In other poems in "The Knife of Love," however, Marty returns more directly to aspects of the theme outlined in "In the Arms of the Family" — family as a humanizing, saving grace in the narrator's life. In "Turning to Meet the World" the speaker in the poem tells

of how he has "dodged the world" through his life in nature up to
the present: "I've made a world of my own / in the palm of a
mountain." Now he sees another potential existence for himself
inside the family, one that seems to provide all the challenges of his
former life and more:

> If this is the last mountain
> I ever climb
> what of it?
>
> There are other ranges, shining
> blue and bright
> in a boy's eye

"The Knife of Love" and *Nobody Danced with Miss Rodeo* itself close
with "The Fording," where the narrator embraces the possibilities
of both family life and the natural world he loves. He watches his
wife and son on horseback sitting in the middle of a creek in the
mountains, talking

> of the things that beautiful women and small boys
> talk of, there where the wind blows the first buds
> of the cinquefoil, and trout skip forward
> from the billowing mud under a horse's foot
> to glitter in the clear again
>
> I would be like those quick gleams
> to be always shining for their eyes and hearts.

Out of his wish to be connected with this vision of his family, the
narrator lights a fire where he stands in a nearby clearing. In
response, with "a whoop, with a shout," his family rides through the
beauty of the wilderness ("over a plain of trembling orange flowers") towards him. The speaker, in an active gesture of acceptance
of those he calls "my living lights, the fire of my days," feels himself
"cry aloud at their fatal beauty." At the close of the poem he is

"running forward to meet them, and surrender." I know of few other contemporary male poets besides Marty who have spoken with such clarity of the life choices that tug at a North American man, nor who have so completely spelled out their acceptance of family joy and responsibility, of the dimensions of fatherhood.

III Dale Zieroth

Love of family and of the wild places of the world, however, are also probed in the poetry of Dale Zieroth. Like Marty, Zieroth takes an unflinching look at the tensions implicit in all life decisions, and especially those connected with marriage and parenting, employment, and the natural environment.

Zieroth's poetic evaluation of the family includes, unlike Marty's, a grappling with his family of origin. "Father," published in Zieroth's first collection, *Clearing*, begins with a moment of intense anger. The father physically shakes the narrator-as-child as if the child were an object ("a sheaf of wheat") or as though one animal is killing another ("the way a dog shakes / a snake"). This sense of overpowering, violent force establishes in a reader a feeling of the awesome power of the father as seen by the young narrator. This feeling is reinforced as "for seven more years" the speaker in the poem watches his father "with his great hands rising and falling / with every laugh, smashing down on his knees." In the poem, too, the speaker *observes*, but the father *acts*. The father's actions are part of a rough, violent world where the farmer-father is observed trimming his fingernails with a knife, "castrating pigs and / skinning deer," and working outdoors for long hours through sun and bitter cold.

In the last stanza, however, we see the father, now grown old, in a different light. He is less active and less competent. We learn that he has given Christmas presents "for the first time," but they are "unwrapped." The father is living on a pension, with the hardness gone from him now that he is no longer involved with heavy physical labour. The "great hands" that once could shake the child or crash down on his knees or work so hard are now "white, soft, / unused hands." Yet the poet indicates that the anger the reader is shown in the first stanza has changed its form, not disappeared. The narrator says the father is "no longer afraid to call his children fools / for finding different answers, different lives." However, the father, as previously described, does not seem to be the sort of man who is "afraid" to point out the shortcomings he sees in his children. Hence there is a mystery to the poem that adds depth to this otherwise straightforward, though gripping, account of an aging parent.

In the final stanza the narrator describes the father "sleeping in the middle / of the afternoon with his mouth open as if there / is no further need for secrets." Perhaps one of these secrets is that the instances of violent behaviour by the father masked an insecurity of some sort when the father was faced with children, or with others of a different temperament or set of beliefs than himself. Or perhaps the father in his active years had some sort of doubts about his life (suggested by the reference to the father's talk with his companions about "the / old times" and their "dead friends"). Whatever the exact nature of these hidden aspects of the father, the portrait depicted is a distressing one of a harsh, primitive power not tamed or civilized but defeated by toil and age.

Zieroth's skills as a craftsman, working and reworking his poems slowly until he obtains precisely the effects he wants, are evident in "Father" as in others. For example, to convey how the father's hard work slowly but inexorably wears him out, the poet in the last line of the second stanza uses mostly single-stress words. The strong, monotonous rhythm thus created helps emphasize the forces steadily hammering at the father: "the work that bent his back a little more each day down toward the ground." And the apparently random line breaks Zieroth uses in the poem ("chokecherry / wine"; "their / youth"; "the same / knife") serve to introduce a tentative, halting effect to the poem's flow. It is as if the narrator is still attempting to come to an understanding about his father, and he relates the events he wishes to describe in a hesitant, uncertain manner. This uncertainty is also underlined in the choice of diction of the poem's concluding stanza. The father's present attitudes are described with qualifiers: "seems," "as if," and again "as if":

> Still, he seems content
> to be this old, to be sleeping in the middle
> of the afternoon with his mouth open as if there
> is no further need for secrets, as if he is
> no longer afraid to call his children fools
> for finding different answers, different lives.

The female side of Zieroth's family of origin is probed in some detail in the poet's third collection, *When the Stones Fly Up*. In "His Mother Laments" the female speaker in the poem — probably the poet's mother — tells of her life after marriage, of leaving her own family behind to come to the new husband's "farm / . . . riddled with his mother, his / knowledge." She speaks of her four children "forming a circle / from out of a circle" and then eventually leaving:

> and they drift past me,
> breaking all the dream I ever had
> and even now I am still
> dreaming them, how they were
> first touched by the midwife's hand, his mother
> pushing gently down, then
> putting a light in the window

The speaker mentions that the last child was, instead, a hospital birth. She feels this experience "made him different, / made him think he can speak for me / (for us, for any of us)." In a nod towards the impossibility of anyone ever knowing fully about the people who are our family of origin, Zieroth concludes the poem by having the speaker question "where in me is he now."

And yet these ancestors are part of who we are, and so the search to understand them is part of understanding ourselves. In *When the Stones Fly Up* Zieroth continues his exploration of the feminine side of his family tree in poems such as "Grandmother's Spring," a consideration of that midwife-grandmother mentioned in "His Mother Laments." "Grandmother's Spring" presents the "sleepy grandchildren" hearing the grandmother summoned in the night when neighbours' wives had complications in birthing. The grandmother is a success at this work: "Babies were her best crop." Yet the world the children enter is that of the fathers: the children "are part of / their father's dream" when they are alive, and even in the act of being born the babies are "shoved and pulled from the darkness and into / their father's bright light." As we have seen from earlier poems like "Father," the patriarchal world of this farming community is one of rigid attempts to control the natural world. Here, in the "father's dream," the wildness in nature is seemingly pacified, regulated:

> green fields bending back to take his work,
> none of the wild oats that stick
> scattered heads above the wheat and
> never follow rows

Also in the dream are "no bloated cows / no young-eating sows / no problems with bulls jumping fences."

Despite the fathers' attempts to impose a human restructuring of nature, though, the natural world seems to belong to the young and the feminine. It is the children who savour the sights of spring: "the first crow," "new grass," "the fields . . . putting on their black robes again," new kittens that appear "out of the barn." Natural growth, rebirth of every sort, is identified with the grandmother: "as she falls, day by day, / her greenness pushes up."

These polarities haunt Zieroth's view of the family. In the background is a male struggle to wrest a living for the family from a natural order identified with feminine strengths of a different sort than rigid control. Domestic life also encompasses tension between conflicting attitudes, emotions, needs, wants. Love of spouse and children is a more intense variant of love of farming, of the land that simultaneously feeds and breaks us. "Beautiful Woman" in *Clearing* sets forth with absolute clarity the love, hate, and resolution that are characteristic of most intimate and meaningful relationships in the poet's world.

In the poem's first stanza the sensual, sexual joys of love are celebrated. The world of the bedroom is fecund and magical: "Fish / swim past the edges of our bed, oceans / in their mouths." The speaker in the poem talks of "this fever to be mad in each other's / warm white skin." There is something primal in this state of being:

> We go down
> like children, we go down into a great moaning
> with silence forgotten and floating through the
>   ceiling
> like balloons. . . .
> See again the sun and bed wet with warm rain.
> Wave after wave it comes, wave
> after wave stones
> break open at our touch, small bones break free and
>   drift
> out of you into me.

But in the second stanza the opposite polarity — anger — appears. The loved one has her list of grievances:

> You tell me
> what it means to wait and work afternoons
> with dishes and floors. You tell me
> my friends who pace and strut ignore you, or notice
> only your sex. How you hate them!

The loved one's rage, however, hurts only the narrator. And he responds in kind: "you will hear me cursing, you will hear me / roaring." In one of the most blistering couplets on spousal hate anywhere in literature, Zieroth's narrator denounces his partner for all time: "The mirror / will fall, history will vomit at your name."

Yet the poem's third stanza provides a synthesis between these two states of exalted passion and deep rage. This synthesis, the speaker in the poem argues, is real life: "In the kitchen / the dishes wait." Ultimately the couple's life together will not depend on extremes of feeling, but on acknowledging these and yet reaching an accommodation:

> Tonight
> we will go deep into our powerful
> bodies again. Or we will do nothing
> and survive just the same.

In this synthesis "both the music and the bruises have gone," and the poem ends with an image of the two-edged nature of ordinary daily life: light that "stains the bed / like wine." The clarity, the enlightenment, that the synthesis provides affects the core of the marriage ("the bed"). Like wine, such a synthesis is acknowledged to contain the potential for both a pleasurable high and destructive behaviours. Inebriation is by definition a state of being out of control, with the resultant possibilities for both ecstasy and harm. The light the couple finds to live by marks their lives together with knowledge of such extremes, the way a wine stain can serve as a momento of intensely good times and/or hurtful ones, too.

As with marriage, the arrival of children is an occasion for the poet to wrestle with poles of emotional response, followed by acceptance of a synthesis. In "Birth," from the poet's second collection, *Mid-River,* the speaker tells of the "resentment and then the guilt" the baby generates in the couple. All has happened as more experienced parents ("they") predict:

> my wife would not love the child instantly
> and both of us would run
> I would be hemmed in like a
> fighter going down for the last time

> I would long for
> a single night's sleep
> the undisturbed dawn   a day away from
> the stink of things   that much time
> without the guilt
> knowing exactly how long
> I'd been away from home   how much
> she needed me

In the second stanza the narrator responds to a more positive part of the prediction: "they said   it gets better." The new father responds to "a smile" from the baby and realizes that he has an important place in his daughter's life. Such a realization frees him to move beyond the darker aspects of parenting:

> After her bottle and her blanket   after
> her mother there is me
> big old man no longer afraid to tell a stranger
> the tiny words of love   love and the need
> to be charged again by something human
> like the morning when her arms go up to me

The third stanza describes the resolution of these extremes when the child is "almost a year." Looking back, the narrator recalls the struggle to accept parenthood, and the wife's primary role in this acceptance: "I did not know / there were babies everywhere and mothers who can / hold us all together." Overall, he concludes, he has grown through the experience of working to resolve his divergent feelings; having a family, he says, "makes me big." And the poem ends with praise for how the arrival of the child has renewed the speaker's sense of what is rewarding about human existence. He talks of how he was present at the instant of her birth, a birth that he realizes now was the beginning of something welcome in his life: "look god she is / alive like her father who stands up inside his eyes and is / delivered to the good world again."

Another birth is the setting for the resolution of conflicting emotional extremes in "Father and Child" from the later collection *When the Stones Fly Up*. Here the child appears surrounded by

> the paramilitary sirens
> of the ambulance drivers, their blue
> uniforms appearing suddenly
> atop the stairs

Whether intentionally or not, the birth takes place at home, leaving the father in the second stanza basically an onlooker:

> and in the doorway
> the father, stunned again by women,
> by the blood on the bed
> the placenta in the bowl
> their cord as tough as garden hose

In this poem the tensions of the situation are both indicated and resolved in the third and final stanza. The work, and accompanying lack of sleep, involved in caring for a new baby are pointed to as the father tends the just-born baby through the night "while his wife sleeps," attempting to "[take] her self back." The father's apprehensiveness about what the child's arrival will mean is suggested by the description of the father having "sunk himself month by month / down into this child," this baby that "stares and stares at him now." The resolution that is ahead is hinted at by the union of father and child in sleep: "At 4 a.m. / with the first light still to come / they sleep, and meet again."

The joys and negative aspects of child-*rearing* are explored by Zieroth in separate poems rather than by striving for a synthesis in one. "The Eyes of the Body Are Not the Eyes of the Mind," from *Mid-River,* is about the pleasure found in showing a child the world. The child asks to be lifted up to see out the window. It is a moment of happiness for the speaker:

> my arms
> fold and lift and hold and now I know
> what they have been made for, why
> they lead out from beside the heart.

The speaker is responding to the way the child is totally absorbed by the world that is so new to her. The ordinary rural sights of horses and ravens the father lifts her up to view "make you stop as if I have shown you a / miracle." Perhaps fuelled by the success of this activity, the narrator at the close of the poem appears to regard the responsibility of parenting, the attempt to introduce the child not only to the wonders of existence but also to its dangers, as within his and his wife's abilities:

> You'll do all right and all we ever do is
> point things out, show you what it's like
> above the crowds, all we can ever do is
> hold you, little spy face,
> keep the world safe another dozen years.

But showing things to the child is a much less successful venture in "Fear of Failure" from the same collection. In this poem the child is five, and the father in the poem is trying to teach her to ski for the first time. The event is frustrating for both father and child:

> she whacks me on the knee
> ski pole on cold bone
> and I grab her and she cries
> and I'm mad now cause I've done that wrong
> and my record for being the kind of father I want to be
> is still too few days.

Even the father's attempts to sort out rationally what has happened fail here:

> later I try to
> explain but I must hold too tightly cause she
> spins away and it's finished for her anyway, she
> decides to take up skating while I
> go over the words again: Look
> Nobody's Good Right Away
> At Anything

The speaker's comment is, of course, ironic, in that his advice applies as much to his own efforts at fathering as to his child's at skiing. But the poem's overall tone reflects the speaker's depression at his failure:

> I lack the drive
> I slide down past the handholds of home
> and I manage and scarcely care today
> where the melting snow goes or takes me or ends.

Another somewhat bleak look at a setback in parenting is described in "Death of the Violin" from Zieroth's fourth collection, *The Weight of My Raggedy Skin*. After four years, a daughter is being allowed to give up violin lessons. The parents accept that the daughter is not particularly interested in studying the instrument. And the parents have no wish to force her to practise her new skills despite the narrator's pride in her accomplishments so far:

> We could no longer continue with
> reminders, because reminders would be
> nagging, and we wanted discipline
> on her part: we wanted her to bring her will
> into play.

As with so many familial behaviours, the wish for violin lessons for the child has its roots in the speaker's family of origin. His father formerly played the violin. The speaker's memories of this are positive ones; he recalls when, under his father's touch,

> the instrument
> became a fiddle, and around him
> guitars and accordions
> filled up the family with their talk.

Here the lost connection with this past is dramatized when, as the daughter practises, the father's old violin, which hangs on the wall, resonates: "just once / that calling note." But the link cannot be sustained: "Then silence / filled up now with rain." The loss of continuity is felt and expressed in angry argument: "And someone's disclaiming all reason / and another's volume rises to the shriek."

Whatever a parent's successes or failures, though, eventually the children grow up and begin their own, ultimately adult life. In "California," also from *The Weight of My Raggedy Skin,* the narrator's daughter is travelling in California, a "country he has never seen." That his child has begun to have experiences that the narrator has not is a measure of how much she has grown from a time when he was the one to introduce her to the world. His life now seems less exotic than hers. On the telephone she tells of palm trees, while he can only speak of domestic banalities, like taking an injured family pet to the SPCA or the price of a needed new muffler for the car. The "real news," he states, is his awareness, presumably sparked by the daughter's trip, of how his life is passing:

> he feels
> a silence come toward him
> now that he has reached
> and found the ground
> nearer than remembered.

The speaker in the poem finds himself irritated with the ordinariness of his daily life, "the clutter / that settles into a house." He compares his static domestic situation to his "travelling" daughter who is discovering things about life that will continue to distance her from the father. As she follows her own life, separate from the family, she "absorbs what makes her strange."

Besides responding to the family, and fatherhood, Zieroth has written equally honestly about his interactions with nature, including working in the outdoors. Nature to Zieroth can be a force that men try to bend to their purposes — as in farming, for example. But even when nature is appreciated for its own beauty, or for how it provides a sense of historical or geologic time, the power of natural forces always includes a potential threat. In "Baptism," from *Mid-River,* the speaker is canoeing with a companion and is fascinated by how the river evokes previous eras. But the strength of the current begins to be overwhelming: "the water takes command," threatening to sweep them against deadfalls. Suddenly in the poem

> water comes up up and the
> snag bends us down until my lungs
> are in the water they are stones and I am
> grabbing for the tree as if it were
> my friend while the current sucks on me and my arms
> go heavy as lead, a scream
> goes dead in my throat, we do not
> belong here

The narrator is pulled underwater

> as if the river is already sure
> how deep it will carry me,
> what it will do with my skin, how it will dissolve
> and burst and thin out the blood

Finally the narrator manages to snag the bank. And when he surfaces, he discovers that his friend has also escaped drowning, "riding the canoe's bottom / like a drunken pea pod."

The narrator speaks of what this "baptism" has taught him. He knows now not to "trust the river" and that "the river is hard, it is / carnal and twists like an animal going blind in the rain." The river's, and by extension (given the similes the poet employs) nature's, purpose and agenda are different than those of humanity. We are in nature, part of nature, but never its master. If we know this, there are amazing rewards:

> Soon our paddles will bite the water but they will not
> break it: our place on earth is rich enough,
> the sudden rush of birdsong, our own
> mid-river laughter as the warmth begins again.

But where people try to make a living from nature, this necessary respect often is ignored. In "Father" Zieroth writes of a farmer eventually worn down by the ceaseless effort to control the natural world. The tourism industry, too, represents a clash between humanity's drive to adapt the natural world to our uses and the wilderness's own processes. In "Coyote Pup Meets the Crazy People in Kootenay National Park," also from *Mid-River*, four employees of the park watch an injured coyote pup die in the back of a warden's vehicle. Although never stated in the poem, it is likely the pup was hit by a car and found by the side of the road, since otherwise it is not clear how the warden would have picked up the injured animal.

Tourists have come to the park to appreciate nature, and ironically their presence leads to the destruction of at least part of what they presumably value. Similarly the men employed by the park are expected to protect the natural world while simultaneously easing (and hence increasing) tourists' destructive access to it. The park employees observing the dying pup seem genuinely sorry at his death: "we / wanted him to run like the wind for the bush." But they are caught up in the contradictions of their own work world. After the death, on their coffee break, they talk shop, "talking / park in the jargon of the civil servant man." Although the ostensible subject of their conversation, their consideration, is nature (the park), the wilderness is spoken of in industrial (i.e., human) terms: "the talk goes wildlife and telex and / choppers   it goes numbers and man-years and / stats." The narrator calls this "nuts" and calls himself and the other employees "crazy people" because of this gap between the reality of the wilderness and their attempts to quantify and control as a means of carrying out their impossible task of preserving both wildness and the comfort of tourists:

> And someone tries to tell me
> what this park really needs
> what this park is really like, but I know already
> it's like a dead coyote pup
> lying out in the back of a warden's truck
> waiting for the plastic bag we're
> going to stuff him in and then we're going to
> shove him in the freezer along with
> the lamb that got it from the logging truck
> along with a half dozen favourite
> birds wiped out by cars, specimens now

The narrator expresses his moral revulsion at what people are doing to the wilderness:

> it was the wrong way to die   in the back of
> a warden's truck   looking at steel
> watched by humans   handled and pitied and
> down on your side in the muck
> a pup   seven months out of the den.

The narrator sees what is beautiful in the world as bound up with the natural; he speaks of "the cold sweet air that comes from the breath / of the animals." But as a person needing to survive economically, he has accepted a job as one of "the crazy people." Coffee break is over and "we hurry to our places / the crazy people and me, we gotta get back to our / paper work."

A glimpse of more morally satisfying work in nature is provided in "Wooding" from the same volume. Here the narrator and a friend have gone out into the beauty of the autumn woods on a Sunday to find winter firewood. In this landscape the devastation caused by people belongs to the past, and nature has already begun the process of redeeming what humanity has wrecked. The speaker in the poem drives in the truck "past the clearing where the portable mill had stood and / left the hump of old sawdust full of / the only young lodgepole around." The wilderness here is regaining its health, its beauty. As the men seek "the perfect tree . . . nutcrackers bobbed in their flight / past the meadow where the elk had grazed and eaten / and already bedded down." Even the men's goal is reached "on the last skid trail." What has been used to harm the forest has been transformed into a source of what is valued: the tree is "dead and clean and dry as a dollar bill."

While the men are returning with their firewood, they fall into a discussion about the problems of human life: "fuel bills and devastation" and fears and promises to do with "the future." However, when they physically reach the human community, their town is overshadowed by the natural beauty they have been part of on this outing: there is snow on Chisel Peak overlooking the town (Invermere, B.C., on Lake Windermere). This positive connection with nature will last, the speaker says: "this winter / our sleep would be warm with the forest."

Even though Zieroth for several years now has lived in North Vancouver, and no longer works outdoors, the natural world continues to be a subject of his poems. The urban poet's relation to nature finds expression in, among other settings, poems about the Manitoba farm and its landscape where he grew up. One of the most humorous and affecting of these Manitoba-based poems is "When My Cows Break Loose" from *When the Stones Fly Up*. The intrusion of rural memories is made startlingly graphic by the first line of the poem: "There are cows in the library again." But the out-of-place cows are more than just a presence; the cows carry with them demands made of the narrator. These animals

> come hulking out of the past and want to be
> pressed into place, like the books
> row on row, or in the stores, mooing softly under
>   muzak,
> bawling at the edge of the fence, hurting

in their bags when I stayed late
at a baseball game, in a neighbor's field

The speaker says his daughter, who "knows little about cows," is "more like her mother than me," whereas he is "more like the cows." These, then, are *his* memories, what defines him apart from his present family. The poem uses humour to speak gently of an aspect of the narrator's life that he feels is currently missing: a link not just with some idealized rural past, but with active participation in the natural world (via chores and other work, as well as a firsthand appreciation of nature).

IV Being Home

For both Zieroth and Marty an active relation to the wilderness, to the natural world, is often paired or merged with the family. I believe this is because both writers view their responses to these aspects of existence as a major part of a struggle to be at home. In order to be at home on this planet, these writers imply, we need to understand its natural processes. And this is not an understanding we will get by merely *looking* at nature, as though examining some object foreign to our being. The natural world is not static: everything wild contributes to change in nature. Yet humans alone have the ability to devastate or diminish the natural environment. We must learn to live, and hence work, in nature in a way that respects the natural processes. For unless we can feel at home in our work in this world, we will never feel at home off the job. The family, too, involves work, but of a different kind: nurturing a relationship between a man and a woman, child-rearing, the 1,001 domestic tasks. How to feel at ease, at home, amid the choices these challenges steadily present us with, is a preoccupation of both writers.

In *Mid-River* Zieroth goes to the basis of life, water, for a long

poem that explores a number of these concerns. In "Columbia" the
narrator traces the lives of the creeks that feed the mighty river, and
speaks of the threats that tourism, and industrial and real estate
development pose to the natural order along these watersheds. In
part, given people's greed for material wealth and lack of awareness
of how our species is connected to natural processes, destructive
change seems inevitable. The creeks

> have heard the rumble of the dams and the
> click-click of the pencils of engineers.
> They are gathered under the wing of the fish hawk.
> They wash the feet of the tourist.
> There is no turning back.

Not only the wild but the human will be dislocated by development:

> the fish will change,
> the roads, the bridges will be
> rebuilt, towns will go under, in the name of
> progress we will watch them
> move their houses out. The clear water will be gone

This dislocation has its roots partly in our own drive for consumer
goods, and partly in the frequent lack of power by the local population to make or even influence decisions. Nature, and those who
oppose development, will literally and metaphorically be "flooded"
by negative changes created by our own needs and by those men
and women who possess authority.

> We will let it be flooded
> and we will do it for our things,
> for our duty to the plastic things
> and we will not want it but we will not
> know how to stop. We will be washed over by television,
> by lawnmowers and trucks and bright lights,
> we will stay plugged in.

The speaker warns the river:

> They are going after you,
> all the good people of the country, they are
> going to make you better. They are going to make you
> serve. And when I ask you
> where are your friends
>   there is only silence.

The speaker's call for action by people on behalf of the Columbia watershed's natural state, or at least on behalf of nondestructive human interaction with the river, is a repeated motif throughout the poem: "Where are the dreamers and the / rebels? Where are the ones who will rage, / the ones who will rage for an end to this thing?" The narrator states that opposition will only arise when people care enough to be angry at what is occurring. He speaks of

> a moment of fury when we
> stand with our children and we block the machines,
> when we tear our page from the maps
> and we drive the consultants
> back to their shame.

In the autumn of 1991, as I was assembling this essay, Zieroth's predictions published ten years previously were coming true in the region of B.C. where I live. Hundreds of women, men, and children stood up to "block the machines" when the watersheds of Hasty Creek and Lasca Creek in the West Kootenays were threatened with road building and, ultimately, development in the form of logging. Many of these people were arrested, but the fight to preserve "clear water" is by no means over. Sid Marty, too, has been part of the struggle to save a watershed, to stop the dam on the Oldman River in southwestern Alberta, near where he has a small ranch. On his 1990 cassette of music, *Let the River Run,* Marty's lyric gifts find effective outlet in the title song. Marty's personification of the river reminds the listener that the Old Man after whom the river is named was a creator spirit of the Indians of the area. The singer calls on the spirit to act on behalf of the river:

> Rise up OldMan
> Though your body is scarred
> Even though your sacred trees
> have fallen to the saw
>
> I've heard tales of power
> You moved the mountains before
> Never was there an hour
> When your people needed you more
>
> Way up high in the Porcupine Hills
> Back when the earth was still young
> And The People were mud in your hands
> You stood all alone with the Sun

The song ends with a prayerlike chant: "Let the river run, let the river run / Let the river run free forever / Let the river run." In the family of all living things we call the biosphere, water is the progenitor. As such it makes a perfect focus for both authors' themes. Zieroth ends "Columbia" with an equally incantatory chant: "Your water will wash our bones. / Your water will cleanse us. / Your water will take us all home."

Being home is the opposite of being in the elsewhere, or nowhere. Yet one of the weird aspects of our strange universe is that you can be at home in the elsewhere even if to an *outside* observer you are invisible, lost in that portion of space-time. I believe the writing of both Marty and Zieroth reflect these authors' efforts to be at ease in the actual here and now, and that what Marty and Zieroth have to say about their struggles has much to teach about a better way to be a human being. I am convinced that, whether out in the elsewhere or arrived, their writing possesses the potential — the same potential as has nature and the family they sing — to "take us all home."

4 FIGHTER IN AMBER: AN APPRECIATION OF MILTON ACORN

When Cy Gonick of *Canadian Dimension* suggested that the death of the poet Milton Acorn be marked by a poetry contest on the theme of "Milton Acorn in Heaven," I was immediately enthusiastic. I felt the topic wide enough — and quirky enough — to encompass poems written in as many moods and themes as the writings of the poet himself: "satirical, political, humorous, lyrical," as the contest announcement said.

Nor did the poetry submitted to *Dimension* prove otherwise. The poems span a range of styles, attitudes, and subject matter; many incorporate the blunt, unswerving look at contemporary society found in Acorn's finest writing. I believe it is a tribute to the scope of Acorn's achievement that the poems written for the contest deal with such a spectrum of his interests, as well as his sometimes crusty personality.

My own reaction to the writer and his words also includes a range of responses. There are poems of his I consider magnificent, with lines I will carry with me my entire life: Acorn's "I shout love," or the image of his mother dragging "her days like a sled over gravel," or the landscape of Acorn's home province of Prince Edward Island that the tourists find so peaceful: "wondering / At the beauty and gentleness / Of the Island countryside, the Island people," these visitors not knowing the place's true history, that "every part of it was laid out for war."

Acorn was one of the first people to show me it is possible to write about work and the working life. The albeit few poems of his about his years as a carpenter include terse lyrics that nevertheless contain humour, like "In Addition":

> In addition to the fact I lost my job for a nosebleed
> In addition to the fact my unemployment
>   insurance stamps were just one week short
> In addition to the fact I'm standing in line at the
>   Sally Ann
> for a breakfast of one thin baloney sandwich and coffee
> In addition to all that it's lousy coffee

And Acorn's work poems can express surprisingly tender feelings, as in his portrait of his friend "The two hundred and fifty pound road foreman / Gone on his liquor" in "I've Gone and Stained with the Colour of Love."

On the other hand, Acorn's emotional problems could make him an unpleasant person to be around. I remember him out of control at a poetry festival in Collingwood, Ontario, during the mid-1970s, roaring abuse at a high school student who had innocently asked some question to which Acorn took inappropriate exception. "I'm going to shoot your head off with a bazooka!" he screamed at the terrified youngster. It took the calming presence (and giant size) of the poet Al Purdy, also at the event, to return Acorn to a semblance of rational behaviour.

I found admirable Acorn's insistence that contemporary poetry should loudly oppose as well as document social injustice. But I also watched with dismay how Acorn's poverty seemed to have an irresistible appeal for many people. These individuals regarded him as the latest incarnation of the Romantic ideal of the poet forced by society's neglect to endure a garret existence. Or else they saw Acorn as the embodiment of a political Romanticism that equates working-class revolution with poverty. I think both ways of seeing Acorn greatly diminish the potential impact of his writing.

Praising Acorn as the solitary neglected artistic genius helps reinforce the stereotype that art is the preserve of rare and eccentric individuals incapable of being understood by the insensitive majority. It follows from this stereotype that the production of art cannot be the activity of normal people like you and me. One effect of this stereotype is that we expect great art to be unintelligible, and sometimes even assume that the less accessible the art is, the better it must be. Another effect of this stereotype is that we describe artists as speaking *for* us, as though we were incapable of articulating for ourselves, by one means or another, what we find important to say. A third consequence of this stereotype is that it encourages indulgence of artists' self-destructive, self-centred, or other antisocial behaviour because, after all, artists are not like other people.

The equation of beneficial social change with poverty ends up proposing that revolution is about self-denial, rather than self-fulfillment, through collective action. This proposal includes the notion that poverty contains some special virtue or purity, that the poor possess a superior moral viewpoint. In reality a long experience of poverty can cripple people emotionally, nutritionally, mentally, et cetera. As the poet Robert Mezey has written, quoting his mother: "Poverty is no disgrace / but it's no honor either."

Only a close friend or biographer of Acorn could tell how much Acorn himself subscribed to these Romantic concepts. But the saddest aspect to linking Acorn with these political and artistic ideas is that neither attitude, despite its posture of defiance, is any threat to the status quo. By suggesting that art is created by a chosen few, Romanticism isolates the artist from the majority of the population. So how could a Romantic artist "speak for" a community when both the artist and the members of that community agree the artist exists apart from men's and women's ordinary lives? Romanticism argues for individual rather than collective solutions to artistic (and societal) problems. Since the root *cause* of such problems is social, however, this position guarantees the irrelevance of any responses the artist may depict in his or her art. And both these Romantic attitudes reinforce the essentially elitist concept of art now entrenched — regardless of the content of an artist's productions.

Similarly the Romantic identification of poverty with revolution isolates a believer in this concept from the goals of trade union and other struggles against social injustice in this century. These battles have been waged, in the words of the slogan of the Industrial Workers of the World, "for more of the good things of life" for a majority of the population. Holding up poverty as the symbol or basis of community or proletarian virtue thus flies in the face of the majority's experiences and aims. Poverty as a goal has not turned out to be a rallying cry capable of inspiring beneficial social change.

Once Acorn was sealed in the amber of his admirers' Romanticism, the sharp cutting edges of his poems were in no position to matter. He accepted the title of "People's Poet," even though it must have been clear even to him that the award was not presented by "the people" in any manifestation but by some of his fellow Canadian *poets*. In actuality this award made him the *"Poet's* People's Poet" — a label with a different significance than the official title. The award was advantageous to the mainstream literary practitioners since these men and women, having assigned socially conscious verse to one chosen individual, were now free to get on with creating "real" poetry. Anybody who has endured literature classes is aware that "real" poetry involves concerns and styles that interest an ever-declining percentage of the population in the art form.

Instead of participating in this arrangement Acorn might have taken a collective rather than an individual approach to art. One such alternative is to encourage people to articulate for *themselves* the conditions of their own lives. The desired result in this case is not the anointing of a "people's poet," but an art form practised at every level of society (as music is today, for example). The aim here is a people of poets. Or, to paraphrase Emiliano Zapata: "A strong people are their own poets."

This goal matches that of the contemporary work writing movement. What Acorn might have written had he endorsed this broader vision can be glimpsed by reading the carpenter poets we are getting now, people such as Clemens Starck of Oregon or, from the women-into-trades movement, Kate Braid of Vancouver.

Despite Romanticism's impact on Acorn, he was unquestionably a pioneer. With considerable energy — sometimes bordering on the manic — he did crowbar a hole in the wall separating literature from the working life that engages the minds, bodies, and most waking moments of the majority of our adult population. Thus he was a forerunner to the new writing about daily work, even if circumstances led him to other concerns than those of the current work writers. Pioneers, after all, make mistakes that their successors are able to learn from, and so avoid.

Acorn's achievement is thus worthy of celebration. To me, the words of his best poems, through their impressive vigour, call for more response than mere appreciation. In these poems his words are like those he refers to in "On Speaking Ojibway":

> Words always steeped in memory
> and hope that makes sure
> by action that it's more than hope.
> That's Ojibway, which you can speak in any language.

Acorn understood that action as well as words is necessary to obtain social justice, to try to build a heaven in this life rather than in the hereafter. This is why it is so intriguing to imagine — as in *Canadian Dimension*'s poetry contest theme — the poet transported to Paradise. And for people like myself, who viewed Acorn's activities on Earth with a mixture of praise and blame, there is the conclusion of his poem on Norman Bethune to remember: "I've set one mark. Let's see some competition. . . ."

5 THE SKIN OF THE EARTH: MY NERUDA

"The skin of the earth" is a phrase from a poem by the Chilean poet Pablo Neruda. Neruda was born in 1904, received the Nobel Prize for literature in 1971, and died in 1973. I chose Neruda's phrase as the first part of my title to acknowledge that although Chile seems an enormous distance from Canada, from British Columbia, the people there inhabit the surface of the same planet as ourselves. The second part of my title emphasizes that, although I intend to explore in this essay Neruda's influence on my writing, I am considering here *my* Neruda, who may bear little or no relation to the real, flesh-and-blood Neruda who lived and accomplished so much, or to the actual, ink-and-paper poems Neruda wrote in Spanish. This possible gap between the true Neruda and my Neruda occurs because I speak and read no Spanish, never met or heard the poet in person, and have never travelled farther south than California. Consequently I will discuss the effect on my literary efforts of Neruda's poems *in English translation,* and of the events of his life as filtered through translators, critics, and other interpreters.

I do share two characteristics with what I understand to be the real Neruda. Like him, I have dedicated my life to scratching down words in that peculiar form we call modern poetry. And like him, I have committed myself to working with others to bring about a fundamental transformation of the social order: to create a society where money is not the sole criterion by which value is judged, and where the elimination of hunger, poverty, and ignorance is considered a more noble and exciting challenge than developing (and using) ever more effective machinery for killing human beings.

No sooner do Neruda and I start to walk along the same road, though, than we have to part company. Neruda's poetry was published in a culture that, by all accounts, treasures that art form as having significance in daily life no less than in the academy. As a result, his poems gained an overwhelmingly positive public reception almost from the start. An enthusiastic and affectionate audience for his poems spread outward from Chile to reach distant continents and eventually to nearly every language and climate on earth. The body of his work, honoured by awards from many countries besides his own, is like a living, breathing giant, as large in stature as the globe itself. His books and readers can be found virtually every place people are able to read.

In British Columbia, on the other hand, poetry is regarded as a mild form of social evil, like those people who still spit on the sidewalk. The dirty practice is probably impossible to stamp out entirely, but society makes clear that it has no sympathy for such an antiquated and irritating vice. A book of poems by a Canadian is likely to sell five hundred copies over three or four years, if the poet is particularly well-known. And of these probably one hundred will be unloaded in B.C. Poetry in Canada is like a brain-dead pygmy, kept clinically alive in the academy by an artificial life-support system. Such mechanical support allows the patient to hover between life and death, but it also contributes to the withering away of the heart and muscles. This situation, I assure you, has a negative effect on the reception of poems written even by an author such as myself!

I also travel a different route than Neruda towards social change. Neruda came to radical politics through his service in the Chilean government's consular corps, to which he was appointed as a very young man in 1927. After service in the Far East, he was posted to Barcelona in 1934 and then Madrid in 1936. In Spain he became very involved with the struggle against the fascists. His experiences, activities, friendships, and political analysis arising out of the Spanish Civil War and its aftermath led him to join the Communist Party of Chile in 1945. He served his party thereafter as senator, activist, and eventually in 1969 as the Party's candidate for president of the republic.

My participation in the North American movements for social

justice has been at the rank-and-file level. The start for me was my presence as a student and then a teacher in the United States in the 1960s. Like many others, I moved quickly from opposition to U.S. involvement in the Vietnamese civil war to a perception of the interconnectedness of war abroad and poverty, racism, sexism, and the wage and factory systems of production at home. Rather than embrace the Communist Party as a means to achieve a just social order, I adopted and continue to hold a set of beliefs that turn out to be similar to ones Neruda held when young and then abandoned. In 1970 Neruda told an interviewer, Rita Guibert, that in his teens he and his generation considered themselves anarchists. The translator here is Frances Partridge. Neruda goes on to say:

> I was translating anarchist books when I was 16. I translated Kropotkin and Jean Graves from the French, as well as other anarchist writers. I read nothing but the great Russian anarchist authors like Andreyev and others. In those days we young anarchists were beginning to find out for ourselves that it was vital for us to join the people's movement, which was also tending toward anarchism at that time. That was the period of the IWW, the Industrial Workers of the World, and almost all the syndicalists belonged to it. (Rita Guibert, *Seven Voices* [New York: Knopf, 1973])

It is this selfsame IWW that I have belonged to and worked in since 1969. It is an IWW today very much smaller than when it functioned in Chile, Australia, and other parts of the world besides North America. But it is a resurgent IWW, since its concepts offer an alternative to the kind of unionism dominant in North America after World War II, a unionism that now seems to be faltering.

Because the IWW is committed to thoroughgoing rank-and-file democracy in the union, and because its members are fervent believers in *decentralized* decision-making, the IWW has very different goals than the Communist Party. For example, the IWW looks with horror on the labour legislation enacted in most nations where the Communist Party has held power. There, all strikes are banned on pain of jail, and to exist unions must be approved by the Party, that is, the state, that is, the *employer.* This labour legislation, you will instantly recognize, also represents the furthest hopes of a member of B.C.'s right-wing Social Credit Party.

To account for this odd coincidence the IWW points to the existence everywhere of economic and social hierarchies: bureaucratic pecking orders that invariably place those who produce the world's goods and services at the bottom of the ladder. In Russia or China no less than here these hierarchies want us to believe democracy should stop the moment we enter the office door or the factory gate. They want us to agree it is *natural* we should obey orders at work — just as once they wanted us to believe that the divine right of kings to command us was natural, and that it was natural to think women were not intellectually or emotionally able to make the decisions required to run a modern state.

But what, you may ask, do these matters have to do with *poetry?* One thing I learned from Neruda is the possibility of integrating one's economic and political outlook with one's poetics. Not to create propaganda, but to demonstrate a poet's revulsion at injustice, the common source from which springs such divergent historical streams as bureaucratic communism and the IWW.

My first encounter with Neruda came via my introduction to Spanish-language poetry more than two decades ago. I had driven south from Vancouver in September of 1966 to pursue graduate studies in writing at the University of California at Irvine, which is located about thirty-five miles south of Los Angeles. Much in California in 1966 was new to me: drugs, light shows, political protest organizations, the semitropical vegetation, beach life with its surfers and days in the sun, the ubiquitous military presence in the skies, in the towns and out at sea. One of the first writers to give a public reading at UC Irvine that fall was the Minnesota poet Robert Bly, the founder of an organization called the American Writers against the Vietnam War.

In Vancouver I had heard a few Canadian poets read, but nothing had prepared me for Bly. He spoke knowledgeably about, and read translations from, poets who wrote in languages other than English.

At the time he was most intrigued by Spanish-speaking poets, many of whom had not been well translated into English. Bly appeared on the stage of a small auditorium at UC Irvine wearing a serape and waving his hands as he recited from Federico García Lorca's *Poet in New York*. He told how the Spanish poet was unhappy in that metropolis, and then García Lorca's time there was finished and he was off to Santiago de Cuba, headed back to the Spanish-speaking culture again. Bly recited García Lorca's poem of joy exuberantly:

> When a full moon rides above Santiago de Cuba
> I'll go to Santiago
> in a carriage of black water
> I'll go to Santiago
> Palm-thatch will sing
> I'll go to Santiago

The reading literally blew my mind. I had no idea there *was* poetry like this — with such energy and delight — nor that poetry could be *performed* like this. I dug into the matter further and discovered that one of Bly's favourite authors was Pablo Neruda. As I studied what Bly wrote about Neruda, I became more and more excited.

Here was I, a student poet involved in protests against the Vietnam War, trying to comprehend how a nation as rich and wonderful as the United States could intervene in an Asian war on the side of a corrupt dictatorship. The 1960s are often romanticized today, but opposition to the war was an extremely unpopular point of view in 1966; a majority of people, including many writers and teachers of writing, were inclined to go along with the *government's* description of what was happening in Vietnam. Yet, as if to bolster our side, especially within the writing community, Bly had translated Neruda's poem to the Venezuelan poet Miguel Otero Silva. This poem was written in 1948 while Neruda was on the run from the police of Chile's then-dictator González Videla. Neruda speaks in the following part of the poem about why he stopped writing like the third century B.C. Greek poet Theocritus:

When I was writing my love poems, which
   sprouted out from me
on all sides, and I was dying of depression,
nomadic, abandoned, gnawing on the alphabet,
they said to me: "What a great man you are,
   Theocritus!"
I am not Theocritus: I took life,
and I faced her and kissed her,
and then went through the tunnels of the mines
to see how other men live.
And when I came out, my hands stained with
   garbage and sadness,
I held my hands up and showed them to the generals,
and said: "I am not a part of this crime."
They started to cough, showed disgust, left off
   saying hello,
gave up calling me Theocritus, and ended by
   insulting me
and assigning the entire police force to arrest me
because I didn't continue to be occupied
   exclusively with metaphysical subjects.

There was more to Bly's translations than this precedent of using poetry to oppose the generals of the world. In an introduction to Neruda, Bly categorizes the poet this way:

We tend to associate the modern imagination with the jerky imagination, which starts forward, stops, turns around, switches from subject to subject. In Neruda's poems, the imagination drives forward, joining the entire poem in a rising flow of imaginative energy. In the underworld of the consciousness, in the thickets where Freud, standing a short distance off, pointed out incest bushes, murder trees, half-buried primitive altars, and unburied bodies, Neruda's imagination moves with utter assurance, sweeping from one spot to another almost magically. The starved emotional lives of notary publics he links to the whiteness of flour, sexual desire to the shape of shoes, death to the barking sound where there is no dog. His imagination sees the hidden connections between conscious and unconscious substances with such assurance that he hardly bothers with metaphors — he links them by tying their hidden tails. He is a new kind of creature moving about under the surface of everything. Moving under the earth, he knows everything from the bottom up (which is the right way to learn the nature of a thing) and therefore is never at a loss for its name. Compared to him, most American poets resemble blind men moving gingerly along the ground from tree to tree, from house to house, feeling each thing for a long time, and then calling out "House!" when we already know it is a house. . . .

Many critics in the United States insist the poem must be hard-bitten, impersonal, and rational, lest it lack sophistication. Neruda is wildly romantic, and more sophisticated than Hulme or Pound could dream of being. He has few literary theories. Like Vallejo, Neruda wishes to help humanity, and tells the truth for that reason. (Robert Bly, ed., *Neruda and Vallejo: Selected Poems* [Boston: Beacon, 1971])

This vision of what a poet could be and do was completely different than any I had encountered. It seemed exactly right to me: you tell the truth, in a century of liars, because you want to help humanity. And to bolster Bly's assessment of Neruda as "wildly romantic," besides political, here is a translation by Alastair Reid of Neruda's "Lazybones":

> They will continue wandering,
> these things of steel among the stars,
> and worn-out men will still go up
> to brutalize the placid moon.
> There, they will found their pharmacies.

In this time of the swollen grape,
the wine begins to come to life
between the sea and the mountain ranges.

In Chile now, cherries are dancing,
the dark, secretive girls are singing,
and in guitars, water is shining.

The sun is touching every door
and making wonder of the wheat.

The first wine is pink in color,
is sweet with the sweetness of a child,
the second wine is able-bodied,
strong like the voice of a sailor,
the third wine is a topaz, is
a poppy and a fire in one.

My house has both the sea and the earth,
my woman has great eyes
the color of wild hazelnut,
when night comes down, the sea
puts on a dress of white and green,
and later the moon in the spindrift foam
dreams like a sea-green girl.

I have no wish to change my planet.

Bly's translation of another part of Neruda's poem to Miguel
Otero Silva exemplifies what Bly means when he suggests a poem
can *help* humanity. Neruda writes:

I remember one day in the sandy acres
of the nitrate flats; there were five hundred men
on strike. It was a scorching afternoon

in Tarapaca. And after the faces had absorbed
all the sand and the bloodless dry sun of the desert,
I saw coming into me, like a cup that I hate,
my old depression. At this time of crisis,
in the desolation of the salt flats, in that weak moment
of the fight, when we could have been beaten,
a little pale girl who had come from the mines
spoke a poem of yours in a brave voice that had
    glass in it and steel,
an old poem of yours that wanders among the
    wrinkled eyes
of all the workers of my country, of America.
And that small piece of your poetry blazed suddenly
like a purple blossom in my mouth,
and went down to my blood, filling it once more
with a luxuriant joy born from your poem.

Romantic effusions and politics are really only two illustrations
of the great scope of Neruda's talents and achievements. The U.S.
translator Stephen Tapscott wrote in 1986 of the limited way people
such as myself first approached Neruda. The following excerpt is
from Tapscott's foreword to his translation of Neruda's *100 Love
Sonnets* (Austin, TX: U of Texas Press, 1986):

> Our received sense of the shape of his career has been some-
> what oddly determined by our own historical circumstances.
> We in the United States discovered Neruda during a period
> of our own turmoil in the 1960s; we seemed to need a poet
> who could be simultaneously affirmative, political, and emo-
> tionally generous, and we found him. In so doing we tended
> to translate primarily the political Neruda (while avoiding for
> the most part his extremely Communist, even Stalinist, works)
> and, subsequently, the lovely early surrealist poems. Neruda's
> early *20 Love Poems and a Song of Despair* and the later *100 Love
> Sonnets* are on the whole his most popular works in South
> America; once we can realign our concept of him a little, to see

him first as a lyrical love poet working from that base, we can
know him more fully and consistently. His more generous
political spirit, his Allendist socialism, and his exuberance for
physical realities and for a populist aesthetics all come from
the same Whitmanian impulses.

I will turn now to the "lovely early surrealist poems" Tapscott
mentions. These come from two books of a larger collection called
Residence on Earth, mainly written, Neruda tells Bly in an interview,
when Neruda was a consul in Burma, Ceylon, Java, and Singapore
between 1927 and 1932. Neruda says he was isolated, lonely, often
living "in an exciting country which I couldn't penetrate, which I
couldn't understand well." So the poetry is very inward-looking.
Here is a translation by Bly and James Wright of a poem called
"Melancholy inside Families":

> I keep a blue bottle.
> Inside it an ear and a portrait.
> When the night dominates
> the feathers of the owl
> when the hoarse cherry tree
> rips out its lips and makes menacing gestures
> with rinds which the ocean wind often perforates —
> then I know that there are immense expanses
>   hidden from us,
> quartz in slugs,
> ooze,
> blue waters for a battle,
> much silence, many ore-veins
> of withdrawals and camphor,
> fallen things, medallions, kindnesses,
> parachutes, kisses.
>
> It is only the passage from one day to another,
> a single bottle moving over the seas,
> and a dining room where roses arrive,

a dining room deserted
as a fish-bone; I am speaking of
a smashed cup, a curtain, at the end
of a deserted room through which a river passes
dragging along the stones. It is a house
set on the foundations of the rain,
a house of two floors with the required number of
  windows,
and climbing vines faithful in every particular.

I walk through afternoons, I arrive
full of mud and death,
dragging along the earth and its roots,
and its indistinct stomach in which corpses
are sleeping with wheat,
metals, and pushed-over elephants.

But above all there is a terrifying,
a terrifying deserted dining room,
with its broken olive oil cruets,
and vinegar running under its chairs,
one ray of moonlight tied down,
something dark, and I look
for a comparison inside myself:
perhaps it is a grocery store surrounded by the sea
and torn clothing from which sea water is dripping.

It is only a deserted dining room,
and around it there are expanses,
sunken factories, pieces of timber
which I alone know,
because I am sad, and because I travel,
and I know the earth, and I am sad.

What I found in poems like "Melancholy inside Families" was
inspiration to fuse Neruda's surrealism with a technique Bly em-

ploys in some poems, a technique sometimes called "deep image" writing. In using the "deep image" strategy, you try to discover and describe or name those objects in the external world that carry the identical emotional charge as internal feelings you wish to convey. A poem of mine from my first collection, *Waiting for Wayman,* is an example of my attempt to link the "deep image" concept to Nerudian surrealism. In this poem I am writing about my emotional realization — as opposed to an earlier intellectual one — of what is wrong with hierarchical parties of the left. Instead of an attraction to these, I felt a pull towards the simple objects we use in daily life. Hierarchies, in power or out, do not really understand objects. Hierarchies are about power, and therefore are remote from those of us who have to exist in them and make the world work despite their constant, stupid, harmful meddling. And we live from cradle to coffin in a swirl of objects accompanying us through time. Only by observing how those objects travelling with us change can we obtain an accurate sense of whether our lives are improving or getting worse. As a nod to Neruda, I call my poem "Melancholy inside Organizations":

> You begin by loving the corporations.
> They betray you. In a fine rain all morning
> you walk through the city.
> A garage door opens. A man's mouth hangs apart.
> You go in.
>
> But his party want everything to be stones.
> If something is moving they want to hit it.
> Everything is simple. They want to die.
> They are overwhelmed by nostalgia
> for the days when all Christians were Saints.
> They are black umbrellas.
>
> You decide it does not mean anything,
> only everything. You stand on the wet sidewalk
> reading the deaths of the Panthers.
> Drops of water roll from your hat.

A dozen or so others are also here.
You go into the paper together. This time
you are very clear:

I cannot escape relating to knives and forks.
To the cold that comes through windows.
To embroidery, elastic bands,
the jammed rooms of the poor
with their piles of mattresses instead of beds.

To clothing stores. Hammers.
The jargon of automobiles.
The body with its tides of blood and water
which cannot be defined or altered by words.
The blood inside the finger.

The deep silence of houses all afternoon.
Gulls. The rainy sea.
Bags of food carried into kitchens
leaving as bags of scraps, crushed packages
and shit. The kind of homes with plants
growing in sunlight on the windowsill.
Sideboard cabinets with glass fronts.

How water is lifted in a bailing tin.
Wet earth. All clutter, and the people
who live in it. Trying on dresses.
Pulling damp air far back in the nostrils.
Relating to forks and spoons.

As the title of my poem implies, I was striving to achieve the
sombre tone found in many of Neruda's surrealist pieces. After the
Second World War, Neruda rejected these early poems for a while
because of this tone. In 1949 the poet gave a speech at a conference
in Mexico City promoting world peace. His talk, translated here by
Joseph Bernstein, was called "Our Duty to Life":

I should like to tell you, for the first time, of an important personal decision I have made. I would not bring it before this gathering if it did not seem to me to be closely bound up with these problems. A short time ago, after traveling through the Soviet Union and Poland, I signed a contract in Budapest for the publication of an anthology of my poetry in the Hungarian language. After signing, I met with the translators and editors. They asked me to pick out, page by page, which poems were to be included in the projected volume. I had seen the thousands of young men and women who had begun to arrive in Hungary from all parts of the earth to take part in the World Youth Festival; I had seen rise up, amid the ruins of Warsaw, the faces of young students who, between classes, were again lifting the shattered pedestal of peace; and I had seen with my own eyes the great buildings built in a few weeks above the ruins of Stalingrad by 25,000 youthful volunteers who had come from Moscow. I heard in those lands a sound like that of bees in an infinite beehive — the sound of pure, collective and boundless joy of the new youth of the world.

That day I glanced through my former books after so many years of not having read them. In the presence of the translators who were waiting for my orders to begin their work, I re-read those pages into which I had put so much energy and care. I saw at once that they were no longer useful. They had grown old; they bore the marks of bitterness of a dead epoch. One by one those pages passed before me in review, and not one of them seemed to me worthy of being given new life. . . .

So I renounced them. I did not want old sorrows to bring discouragement to new lives. I did not want the reflections of a system which had driven me almost to despair to deposit on the rising towers of hope the terrible slime with which our common enemies had muddied my own youth. I did not give permission for a single one of those poems to be published in

the people's democracies. What is more, today when I have
come back to these American lands of which I am a part, I tell
you that here too I do not wish to see those poems reprinted.
(*Let the Railsplitter Awake and Other Poems* [New York: Masses and
Mainstream, 1950])

Luckily for us Neruda later changed his mind, and these poems
have stayed in print both in Spanish and in translation. Once
Neruda's poems become more outward-looking, though, the poet
combines his former close attention to the inward life with subjects
from our ordinary external existence. One area he is a master of
is poems about specific objects. I became interested in such poems
after some years spent working where objects are made: first as a
member of what were called "hippie-labour" crews rebuilding the
Gastown area of Vancouver, and later in a Burnaby factory that
assembled motor trucks. The following poem of Neruda's about
an object is probably my favourite of his. Here the poet stares at
the plump, rounded foot of a baby and notices it does not look
anything like the foot of an adult. The poem is called "To the Foot
from Its Child," and like "Lazybones," is originally from *Extravagaria,* a collection published in 1958. The translation is by Alastair
Reid.

> The child's foot is not yet aware it's a foot,
> and would like to be a butterfly or an apple.
>
> But in time, stones and bits of glass,
> streets, ladders,
> and the paths in the rough earth
> go on teaching the foot that it cannot fly,
> cannot be a fruit bulging on the branch.
> Then, the child's foot
> is defeated, falls
> in the battle,
> is a prisoner
> condemned to live in a shoe.

Bit by bit, in that dark,
it grows to know the world in its own way,
out of touch with its fellow, enclosed,
feeling out life like a blind man.

These soft nails
of quartz, bunched together,
grow hard, and change themselves
into opaque substance, hard as horn,
and the tiny, petalled toes of the child
grow bunched and out of trim,
take on the form of eyeless reptiles
with triangular heads, like worms.
Later, they grow calloused
and are covered
with the faint volcanoes of death,
a coarsening hard to accept.

But this blind thing walks
without respite, never stopping
for hour after hour,
the one foot, the other,
now the man's,
now the woman's,
up above,
down below,
through fields, mines,
markets and ministries,
backwards,
far afield, inward,
forward,
this foot toils in its shoe,
scarcely taking time
to bare itself in love or sleep;
it walks, they walk,
until the whole man chooses to stop.

And then it descended
underground, unaware,
for there, everything, everything was dark.
It never knew it had ceased to be a foot
or if they were burying it so that it could fly
or so that it could become
an apple.

Previously Neruda had published three collections of poems just
about objects. These were called *Elemental Odes* and appeared in 1954,
1956, and 1957. The objects Neruda depicts include salt, the air, a
wristwatch . . . even his socks! Here is a poem of mine about an object.
It is set in the motor truck factory I mentioned earlier. I am considering
the three-quarter inch bolts we employed to attach grilles to the front
of the fibreglass hood shells. The poem is named after the hood line's
partsman in those days, so it is called "Neil Watt's Poem."

At first metal does not know what it is.

It has lived so long in the rock
it believes it is rock.
It thinks as a rock thinks: ponderous,
weighty, taking a thousand years to reach
the most elementary of hypotheses, then
    hundreds more years
to decide what to consider next.

But in an instant the metal is pulled into the light.
Still dizzy with the astounding speed
with which it is suddenly introduced to the open air
it is processed through a concentrator
before it can begin to think how to respond.
Not until it is hurtling along on a conveyer belt
is it able to inquire of those around it
what is happening?
We are ore, is the answer it gets.

A long journey, in the comfortable dark. Then
   the confusing
noise and flame of the smelter, where the ore
feels nothing itself, but knows it is changing
like a man whose tooth is drilled under a
   powerful anaesthetic.
Weeks later, the metal emerges as a box full of bolts.
What are we? it asks. *Three-quarter-inch bolts.*

The metal feels proud about this. And that is a feeling
it knows it has learned since it was a stone
which in turn makes it feel a little awed.
But it cannot help admiring its precise hexagonal
   head
the perfectly machined grooves of its stem.
Fine-threaded, someone says, reading the side of
   the box.
The bolt glows, certain now it is destined for some
   amazing purpose.

Then it comes out of its box and is pushed
first into a collar, *a washer,* and then
through a hole in a thin metal bar.
Another washer is slipped on, and something
is threaded along the bolt, something else
that is made of metal, *a nut,* which is whirled in tight
with great force. The head of the bolt
is pressed against the bar of metal it passes through.
After a minute, it knows the nut around itself
holds a bar of metal on the other side.

Nothing more happens. The bolt sits astonished
grasping its metal bars. It is a week before it learns
in conversation with some others

it is part of a truck.

I hope it is clear the extent to which my writing has made use of Neruda's poems in translation. I once tried to exorcise this possession of my consciousness by his, by writing a poem called "Influences."

> I sit down at my desk
> — and it turns into Pablo Neruda!
> His stout face stares thoughtfully
> up from between my pencils.
> I say to him: *Please. I want to get on with it.*
> *On with being Wayman, with my own work.*
> *Vanish. Vamos!* And he goes.
>
> But just then my chair feels uncomfortable.
> I jump up and look. Neruda again.
> *Pablo,* I tell him. *Please, I insist.*
> *Leave me alone. I've got to do it.*
> *Back to your Chile. Get south.*
> *Sud! Sud! Leave Vancouver to me.*
>
> And he goes. I draw out my papers,
> my scribbles. Scratching my beard.
> I pore over a fine adjustment,
> searching for the perfectly appropriate sound.
> Then I notice the curtain
> leaning over my shoulder.
> "I'd do it this way," it says, pointing.
> "Change this word here."
>
> *Neruda,* I say, getting real mad.
> *Flake off. Go bother Bly.*
> *Teach all the poets of California.*
> While I'm talking to him like this
> he changes from being my curtains
> to a pen. And I see his eyes twinkle
> as they fall on my typewriter.

Then, I get cagey.
I'll be back in a minute, I tell him
and leave, carefully shutting him
inside the room.
Out on my porch, in the cold air
I see the North Shore mountains behind the City.
I'm alone now, shivering.
There is no sound over the back yards
but traffic
and a faint Chilean chuckle.

Despite my attempt in the above poem to free myself from Neruda, I have continued to write poems utilizing a Nerudian subject area, form, mood, or tone.

Neruda often praises wholeness, inclusiveness, as in "Too Many Names" (also from *Extravagaria*), where he uses the phrase "the skin of the earth." He contrasts such a planetary vision with the narrower outlooks implied by the existence of countries. Out of respect for the poet's adoption of an all-encompassing viewpoint, I will briefly describe the darker side of my experiences with him. To begin with, obviously I am at the mercy of his translators. People who know Spanish have told me that some of the poems I particularly like in English are not very good translations of what Neruda wrote. But I also know that some translators of Neruda — accurate or not — do not produce very interesting poetry in English. For years much translation of his poetry was done in the U.S. by Ben Belitt, whose work is particularly unpoetic to my ears. Belitt also displays a fault I observe in some other translators: what I consider unnecessary changes. Glancing at the Spanish text that usually accompanies a translation, I note the poet will use the Spanish word for "stone," for example, three or four times. The translators I do not care for have an irresistible urge to alter this repetition of the word "stone," a usage I believe the poet intended. Instead of this repetition we are given variations on "stone,"such as"rock"or"boulder,"for no apparent reason. This point may be minor, but once I am aware of such a thing occurring in a translation, I can never quite relax about the accuracy of the rest of the poem.

A second difficulty I have with Neruda I have already touched on: his association with a hierarchically organized political party. Neruda's involvement with the Communist Party includes the Stalinist period. In Neruda's *Memoirs,* published posthumously, the poet states that "in several aspects of the Stalin problem, the enemy was right." But it is one of the paradoxes of Neruda that although he can write about the loss of freedom represented by a child's foot having to go into a shoe, he turned a blind eye throughout his life to the Soviet Union's treatment of dissidents, including dissident writers.

In Neruda's address on receiving the Nobel Prize, however, he says he can live with whatever accusations any of us might direct at him. This translation is by the Nobel Committee.

> The truth is that, even if some or many consider me to be sectarian, barred from taking a place at the common table of friendship and responsibility, I do not wish to defend myself, for I believe that neither accusation nor defense is among the tasks of the poet. When all is said, there is no individual poet who administers poetry, and if a poet sets himself up to accuse his fellows, or if some other poet wastes his life in defending himself against reasonable or unreasonable charges, it is my conviction that only vanity can so mislead us. I consider the enemies of poetry are to be found not among those who practice poetry or guard it, but in mere lack of agreement in the poet. For this reason, no poet has any considerable enemy other than his own incapacity to make himself understood by the most forgotten and exploited of his contemporaries, and this applies to all epochs and in all countries. (Pablo Neruda, *Toward the Splendid City* [New York: Farrar, Straus, and Giroux, 1974])

And rather than enter into polemics for or against socialist realism in art, as favoured by Stalin and by other Party officials since, Neruda in his Nobel lecture has this to say about form in poetry:

> From the matter we use, or wish to use, later on there arise obstacles to our own development and to future development. We are led infallibly to reality and realism, that is to say to become indirectly conscious of everything that surrounds us and of the ways of change, and then we see, when it seems to be late, that we have erected such an exaggerated barrier that we are killing what is alive instead of helping life to develop and blossom. We force upon ourselves a realism which later proves to be more burdensome than the bricks of the building, without having erected the building which we had regarded as an indispensable part of our task. And, in the contrary case, if we succeed in making a fetish of the incomprehensible (or a fetish of that which is comprehensible only to a few), a fetish of the exclusive and the secret, if we exclude reality and its realistic degenerations, then we find ourselves suddenly surrounded by an impossible country, a quagmire of leaves, of mud, of cloud, where our feet sink in and we are stifled by the impossibility of communicating.

In reference to quagmires, the third difficulty I have with Neruda concerns the translated version of the poet's *Memoirs*. I found this book to be quite disturbing. Previously I had very much enjoyed most of Neruda's prose that I had read, which was mainly his responses to interviewers' questions. For example, in the 1970 interview with Rita Guibert that I referred to earlier, she attempts to get Neruda to admit whether he would rather achieve the presidency of Chile or the Nobel Prize, the latter being administered by the Swedish Academy. At the time of Guibert's interview Neruda was in the running for both the presidency and the prize. His answers are the perfect response.

You have been a candidate several times for the Nobel Prize. Could the presidency affect in any way the decision of the Swedish Academy?

That question should be put to the Academy, not to me, and needless to say the Academy wouldn't answer.

If you had to choose between the presidency and the prize, which would you choose?

There's no question of deciding between such illusions.

But supposing the presidency and the prize were put on the table in front of you?

If they were put on the table in front of me I should go and sit at another table.

When Guibert, in the best English department professorial style, tries to question the poet on his use of *symbols,* Neruda's answers would be cheered by English students everywhere.

Some symbols keep recurring in your poetry, for instance, the sea, fish, birds . . .

I don't believe in symbols. Those are material things. The sea, fish, and birds have material existence for me. I depend on them just as I depend on daylight. The word "symbol" doesn't express my thought exactly. Some themes persist in my poetry, are constantly reappearing, but they are material entities.

Like flames, wine, or fire.

We live with flames, wine, and fire also. Fire is part of our life in this world.

Doves, guitar — what do they mean?

A dove means a dove and a guitar is a musical instrument called
a guitar.

Memoirs, unfortunately, lacks such modesty and wit. In their place
we read of various egocentric "escapades" involving women, such
as the Argentine poetess Neruda brags of seducing atop a swimming
pool diving tower while invited for dinner to the estate of a million-
aire. And there are incidents such as a speech in a coal mining
district at a political meeting attended by ten thousand miners.
Here is Hardie St. Martin's translation:

> The speaker's platform was very high and from it I could make
> out that sea of blackened hats and miners' helmets. I was the
> last speaker. When my name and my poem ("New Love Song
> to Stalingrad") were announced, something extraordinary oc-
> curred, a ceremony I can never forget.

> As soon as they heard my name and the title of the poem, the
> huge mass of people uncovered their heads. They bared their
> heads because, after all the categorical and political words that
> had been spoken, my poetry, poetry itself, was about to speak.
> From the raised platform I saw that immense movement of hats
> and helmets: 10,000 hands went down in unison, in a ground
> swell impossible to describe, a huge soundless wave, a black
> foam of quiet reverence.

A passage like the above one, where mass self-abasement of the poor
is *praised,* made me wonder for a time if the English-language
version of *Memoirs* is a fake. Could it have been circulated perhaps
by the CIA or the Chilean police to destroy Neruda's growing
reputation in North America, now that the poet is unable to defend
himself?

Neruda perished in the aftermath of the 1973 coup in which the
Chilean armed forces, as the Polish armed forces were to do in 1981,
declared a state of war on their own people. The army in Chile
overthrew the elected government of Salvador Allende, a government

Neruda had worked to elect. The army murdered Allende along with thousands of other Chilean men and women, and imprisoned thousands more under frightful conditions. My uncle, Alexander Wayman, who speaks Spanish after living many years in Mexico, translated for me an interview with Neruda's widow. It was published in the Mexico City newspaper *Excelsior* and concerns the poet's last days. I turned the account into a poem, "The Death of Pablo Neruda," which begins with the couple at their home at Isla Negra, a beach resort on the seacoast about forty kilometres south of Valparaiso.

On the 11th of September, *his wife said,*

there was no sign of illness. It was his custom
to be up for the early morning news and then
after breakfast to read through the newspapers
before beginning work. In France
some days before Pablo received the Nobel Prize
he was operated on for his prostate
and during surgery they discovered the tumor was
   malignant.
But though he never knew this — the doctors
asked me not to tell him — it was felt
the cancer was contained and operable and he
   would live
many years. His own doctor, Roberto Vargas Salazar,
said he would live at least six years and probably die
of something besides cancer, as his was well controlled.

On the 11th he watched TV and heard the radio
   bulletins
all day. It hit him very hard. The next day
he woke up with a fever. I called the doctor in Santiago
— we were then living at Isla Negra — and he
ordered some injections. But the nurse who was
   to give them

could not get through to us. She lived in a village
only five or six miles away, but the soldiers
would not let her pass for two days.

His fever did not diminish. We tried to call
friends in Santiago to find out what was
   happening
but they had already been arrested or gone into hiding.
The doctor had said on the phone not to let Pablo
hear what was happening, but he had a radio
right by his bed and heard everything they reported
including President Allende's last broadcast.
Salvador was a great friend of his; sometimes at
   Isla Negra
he would arrive unexpectedly: there would be a
   great noise
and it would be the president's helicopter descending.
He would stay for supper and they would talk.
   Salvador was planning
a big celebration for Pablo's 70th birthday next July
with guests invited from all over the world. Pablo
was working at this time on six books of poems,
   simultaneously,
and his memoirs, which his publisher in Buenos Aires
intended to bring out on his birthday.

On the 18th, some friends were able to reach the house
who told him what took place in Santiago.
This was very bad for him. He was very ill in the
   evening
and the next day I called an ambulance to take him
to the clinic in Santiago. Because of the trouble
   the police made
it took quite a while for the ambulance to get to us.
As we approached the city, we found the police
were checking everyone. I told them

this was Pablo Neruda in the ambulance, who is very ill.
They acted as though they had not heard me.
They made me leave his side and I was checked. This
affected him very much. When I got back in
I saw there were tears in his eyes; it was the first time
in my life I saw Pablo cry. I told him
not to make so much of it, they were checking
everybody. All this time
I did not think he was really badly off
but that it was mostly the fever, which he had had
    before.
But Pablo was broken inside.

When we got to the clinic, the place was almost
    deserted.
Pablo's doctor had been arrested, but we got
another doctor. I learned that my house in Santiago
had been attacked by the soldiers and burned:
this happened while the government was saying
they would protect Neruda's property. On the 20th,
the ambassador of Mexico came to the clinic
and told Pablo that the Mexican president, Luis
    Echeverría,
was sending a plane to take him there.
Pablo refused to go. We tried to convince him
that he had to leave, but he still said no.
We went outside the room, and the ambassador
told me I should tell him about the house.
We went back inside and I explained we could no
    longer stay.
At last he agreed to go. I left him to go back to
    Isla Negra
to get some of our possessions, returning on the 22nd.
I discovered that while I was away, despite a guard
    at the door,

some people had been in and told him what
   happened
to friends of his: all of this was very bad, Victor Jara,
one of his closest friends, was dead. Even our chauffeur,
who took no part in politics, was in jail
simply because he was our driver. That night

Pablo became delirious, crying out
"They are shooting them. They are shooting them."
I had the nurse give him an injection of tranquilizer
which I had in my purse. He slept
all night, and all the next day. At 10:30 at night
on the 23rd, while I was with him,
he had a convulsion and his heart stopped.
He passed from sleep to death; he did not suffer.

I will conclude with Neruda's own voice, still able to go on
speaking to us across the blackness. This excerpt is from his Nobel
lecture and contains his thoughts on the art form he loved:

I believe that poetry is an action, ephemeral or solemn, in
which there join as equal partners solitude and solidarity,
emotion and action, the nearness to oneself, the nearness to
mankind and to the secret manifestations of nature. And no
less strongly I think that all this is sustained — man and his
shadow, man and his conduct, man and his poetry — by an
ever wider sense of community, by an effort which will forever
bring together the reality and the dreams in us because it is
precisely in this way that poetry unites and commingles
them. . . .

From all this, my friends, there arises an insight which the poet
must learn through other people. There is no insurmountable
solitude. All paths lead to the same goal: to convey to others
what we are.

Finally, from Neruda's 1961 book *The Stones of Chile,* a poem translated by Alastair Reid called "I Will Come Back":

> Some time, man or woman, traveller,
> afterwards, when I am not alive,
> look here, look for me here
> between the stones and the ocean,
> in the light storming
> in the foam.
> Look here, look for me here,
> for here is where I shall come, saying nothing,
> no voice, no mouth, pure,
> here I shall be again the movement
> of the water, of
> its wild heart,
> here I shall be both lost and found —
> here I shall be perhaps both stone and silence.

6 AN ASPIRIN AS BIG AS THE SUN: POETRY AND POLITICS

My fascination with political poetry originated as much with my participation in groups working for social change as with writing and reading poems. Because my involvement in political movements began during the late 1960s, I will start by focusing on that era. Then I will consider the changes in my ideas since.

However, I discovered one fundamental aspect of political poetry before I ever became an activist. This knowledge dates from when I entered the University of British Columbia in 1962. I was seventeen, and I was a rather immature seventeen. I had been allowed to skip a grade in elementary school and thereafter was younger than my classmates and so pretty much a social misfit. Like many people, I had begun to write poetry in high school. I had discovered a book about the beat poets in San Francisco and Venice, California, that included poems that did not rhyme or use regular metre. Although I grasped very little of what these poems were saying, suddenly poetry seemed like something even I could use to express my solitary thoughts and feelings.

In my first months at university I attended all the poetry readings I could. I remember being at a noon hour reading where some fourth-year student poets were performing. Their poems were mainly about living alone in small rooms and about the poets' various adventures and misadventures with the opposite sex. Since at the time I was still living at home and had almost no experience with the opposite sex, I was vaguely aware that although such poetry might mean something to me in the future, at present it did not affect me at all. Whatever poetic craft was displayed or absent, these

literary creations depicted situations that were outside my understanding. Nor could I even *imaginatively* enter into the worlds these
poems portrayed. Nothing in my life up to that point had given me
the intellectual or emotional resources to respond to these poems
in any meaningful way.

I believe the same limitation applies to political poetry. I first
became absorbed in reading and writing political poetry years later
when I was drawn into active opposition to the U.S. military presence in Vietnam. Prior to that, poems on political themes I had
glanced at just did not mean very much to me. Thus I have never
found it surprising that somebody who has not taken much of a role
in social struggles should consider political poetry lacking in interest or merit. Like the seventeen-year-old Tom Wayman, these people are reading or listening to poetry based on situations or events
that are very distant from what these men and women have to date
encountered.

No wonder, then, that the standard themes of English-language
poetry are love, death, and nature, and that politics is regarded in
some people's minds as a less important or second-rate topic for
serious poems. Partly this attitude is a consequence of which poems
are authorized for the curricula of high school and university
English classes. But it is also true that even the most isolated or
insulated human lives will encounter and respond to emotions of
love, to a fear or observation of death, and to the pleasures and
perils of nature. My mission as a writer has been to add the subject
of work to these standard themes of love, death, and nature, since
I argue that no human being can escape the consequences of how
daily work is organized in her or his society during her or his time
alive. Yet it remains possible for somebody to go through life
seemingly removed from *politics:* in a fog, in an ivory tower, in a
closet. To such people political poetry will appear remote and
lacking in emotional or intellectual significance when compared to
poetry dealing with the usual and approved themes.

My own engagement with political movements, and delight in
the best of the poetry that accompanied these, started after I drove
down from Vancouver to attend the University of California at

Irvine in 1966. While doing graduate studies in English and writing at UCI, I began to participate in the student wing of the movement against the U.S. role in the Vietnam War. Specifically I became active with the local chapter of the Students for a Democratic Society (SDS). The chapter at Irvine was not very large nor at first very militant. But I remained an SDS member as the local organization developed because the analysis of society presented by various SDS members and pamphlets made sense to me. This analysis argued that the war in Southeast Asia was not an aberration of U.S. society but was rooted in basic U.S. social and economic structures, activities and attitudes, including capitalism's need to expand, racism, and the wage and factory systems of production. As a Canadian, I became intrigued, too, with considering the ways Canadian society does and does not reproduce U.S. models of social and economic organization.

The political poems I was most interested in at this time mirrored my expanding involvement in anti-Vietnam War activities and my growing awareness of the interconnectedness of many social evils. The political poetry that was most important to me then was woven of four threads that spun out from my own attempts to master the craft of poetry while also taking part in various types of political action. These four threads consisted of: first, poems that examined North American society and revealed its attitudes to a number of social issues; second, guerrilla poems from Third World liberation movements; third, the fact that the leaders of North Vietnam and China were themselves poets; and, finally, poems arising out of past and current political and economic struggles on this continent.

It will be evident from what I have said so far that when I speak of political poems I mean poetry that deals with social questions and social change, at home or abroad, and not *electoral* politics. Our high school and media definitions of politics are almost entirely limited to the world of mainstream political parties — whether this or that party, or party member, gets elected and by how much. But I have yet to see a serious contemporary U.S. or Canadian poem that praises one political party while it condemns another — the standard fare of speeches by candidates for electoral office, and of the political analysis provided by the electronic and print media. An individual party leader may be attacked in a poem, for example a U.S. president or Canadian prime minister or a member of their cabinet. But such opposition expressed in a poem invariably has to do with *moral,* and not electoral, questions. It is as if the poets implicitly understand that North American electoral party politics have *nothing* to do with the larger issues of our common existence.

A visit by Robert Bly to UC Irvine in the autumn of 1966 introduced me to the first thread in the weave of what came to represent political poetry to me. Bly had been one of the organizers of a group called The American Writers against the Vietnam War.

I should emphasize that, at the time, the movement against the Vietnam War was very much a minority in U.S. society. A substantial majority of the population believed what the government said about the reasons for U.S. military involvement in Southeast Asia. Yet the war was also a daily presence in that part of Southern California where UC Irvine is. Jet fighters and helicopters from the Marine Corps bases at El Toro and Camp Pendleton constantly flew overhead. In the beach cities and towns, off-duty soldiers were everywhere, easily recognizable by their very short haircuts. Page three of the *Los Angeles Times* listed daily the names and hometowns of between three and six soldiers from Southern California killed in Vietnam the previous day.

On campus the young men talked constantly about the draft. Their conversations dealt with student deferments, friends they knew from high school who had been called up, the possibility of alternate service in the National Guard or Coast Guard. The war even put a specific pressure on faculty. To fail a male student might result in his being kicked out of university, leading to his immediate vulnerability to the draft, service in Vietnam, and possible injury or worse. The D a professor assigned to a male student on a midterm exam could ultimately signify that young person's Death.

Bly brought to UC Irvine copies of a book called *A Poetry Reading against the Vietnam War,* edited by himself and David Ray and published by Bly's The Sixties Press that year. This small anthology of poems and prose by Americans and others collectively gave the impression of a nation with something amiss at the core. Included in the anthology is Louis Simpson's poem "The Inner Part," which describes how after World War II "for the first time in history / Americans were the most important people." Despite this development, the speaker in Simpson's poem says:

> When their daughters seemed as sensitive
> As the tip of a fly rod,
> And their sons were as smooth as a V-8 engine —
>
> Priests, examining the entrails of birds,
> Found the heart misplaced, and seeds
> As black as death, emitting a strange odor.

Such poems matched Bly's sense of despair — and outrage — over U.S. intervention in Vietnam. In the poems Bly was writing himself around this time, published in 1967 in his collection *The Light around the Body,* he captures this unhappy malaise, what he terms in one poem "a bitter fatigue, adult and sad." Bly's poem "The Great Society" takes its title from then-U.S. President Lyndon B. Johnson's campaign promise for America. The poem begins: "Dentists continue to water their lawns even in the rain; / Hands developed with terrible labor by apes / Hang from the sleeves of evangelists."

Bly was particularly angered by the U.S. armed forces' practice in Vietnam of announcing each day how many of the enemy had supposedly been killed. Speaking at UC Irvine, Bly told how when he served in World War II this practice of releasing a daily body count was not followed. He stated that the body count represented an obsession with numbers gone mad, combined with a contempt for Asian men and women as human beings. His poem on this practice is called "Counting Small-boned Bodies":

> Let's count the bodies over again.
>
> If we could only make the bodies smaller,
> The size of skulls,

> We could make a whole plain white with skulls in
>   the moonlight!
>
> If we could only make the bodies smaller,
> Maybe we could get
> A whole year's kill in front of us on a desk!
>
> If we could only make the bodies smaller,
> We could fit
> A body into a finger-ring, for a keepsake forever.

Bly believed that the racism implicit in such attitudes towards Asians has historical roots. He claimed that since the near-destruction of the American Indians during the westward expansion of the U.S., Americans have wanted to repeat this crime against every other people on the planet who, like the Indians, have black hair. His poem on this idea is called, simply, "Hatred of Men with Black Hair." The last two stanzas are:

> We have violet rays that light up the jungles at
>   night, showing
> The friendly populations; we are teaching the
>   children of ritual
> To overcome their longing for life, and we send
> Sparks of black light that fit the holes in the
>   generals' eyes.
>
> Underneath all the cement of the Pentagon
> There is a drop of Indian blood preserved in snow:
> preserved from a trail of blood that once led away
> From the stockade, over the snow, the trail now lost.

The concept that hair colour could in part be responsible for U.S. involvement in a land war in Asia seems absurd at first glance. But Bly's strange pronouncements often caused his listeners to rethink their preconceptions. One of the worst aspects of living in

North America, narcotized by advertising, television, and daily newspapers, is the way people become numbed out. Thinking of any kind seems decidedly unpleasant compared to going along with the flow, seeking whatever advertised pleasures or ideas are repeatedly and enticingly put before us to be consumed. Concepts like Bly's shook up people's way of seeing the world. If you *didn't* agree that hair colour was responsible for the U.S. military presence in distant Vietnam, what *did* you believe was the cause? I am convinced Bly was serious about his notions, but the result of the strong poetry he wrote, and helped to anthologize, was that it forced those who listened to him, however sceptically, to reconsider their *own* ideas about North American society and its discontents.

Through poems like Bly's I saw that poetry and poets could raise issues and generate critical thinking not just about *literary* issues, as we had been shown in high school and university (such as the poet's use of form, choice of images, et cetera). Instead, poets could induce thinking about vital social issues like resistance to an unjust war. Thus it was partly because of Bly that I first formulated for myself the concept that one vital task for writers is to help serve as the self-appointed conscience of a community. Obviously this undertaking will never be popular. Nobody likes her or his conscience. And yet the importance of a conscience appears undebatable. In any case, I already was aware that writers in North America, with very few exceptions, are far from popular! So the writer's task of representing a society's conscience seemed to me then — as it does still — to combine virtue with necessity.

This self-selected role for authors is a link to the second thread in the web of political poetry that I first responded to: the writings of Third World guerrilla poets. The availability of these poems in translation was significant to me because the existence of Latin American, African, and other liberation movements helped confirm my new understanding that the Vietnam War was not an isolated occurrence. I now saw Vietnam as only an especially prominent part of a pattern of events happening around the world. I also discovered that, like those of us engaged in opposing the U.S. intervention in Vietnam, these guerrillas had *chosen* to become involved in the social struggle in their countries. Like antiwar and social change activists in North America, the guerrillas found a situation in their nation so odious that they felt compelled on moral grounds to participate in movements and organizations dedicated to fundamentally altering that situation for the better. Of course, unlike ourselves, the guerrillas had taken up arms to accomplish their goals. Yet the repression our counterparts faced on a daily basis made such a response understandable.

But the poems of these guerrilla writers seemed at times to speak for us in North America as well as to their own societies. After many arguments with professors and fellow students about the war in Southeast Asia, and about the university's complicity in the war effort abroad and in racism and other social problems at home, I found it a joy to read Otto René Castillo's poem "Apolitical Intellectuals." Castillo had been a student activist in Guatemala, as well as a prize-winning young poet. He joined the Revolutionary Armed Forces in 1966 and was captured and tortured to death in March 1967 at the age of thirty-one. Yet Castillo's poem set in Guatemala contains a frustration similar to that we felt trying to convince smug academics that they, too, were involved with the horrors the U.S. government was perpetrating in Vietnam and in America. This translation of "Apolitical Intellectuals" is by Margaret Randall:

I

One day
the apolitical
intellectuals
of my country
will be interrogated
by the simplest
of our people.

They will be asked
what they did
when their nation died out

slowly,
like a sweet fire,
small and alone.

    No one will ask them
about their dress,
their long siestas
after lunch,
no one will want to know
about their sterile struggles
with "the idea
of the void"
no one will care about the way
they ontologically acquired their funds.
They won't be questioned
on Greek mythology,
or about the self-disgust they felt
when someone within them
began to die
the coward's death.
They'll be asked nothing
about their absurd
justifications
born in the shadow
of the total lie.

II

    On that day
the simple men will come,
those who had no place
in the books and poems
of the apolitical intellectuals
but daily delivered
their bread and milk,
their tortillas and eggs,

those who mended their clothes,
those who drove their cars,
who cared for their dogs and gardens,
and worked for them,
and they'll ask:
"What did you do when the poor
suffered, when tenderness
and life
burned out in them?"

III

Apolitical intellectuals
of my sweet country,
you will not be able to answer.

A vulture of silence
will eat your guts.
Your own misery
will gnaw at your souls.
And you will be mute
in your shame.

The Latin American guerrilla poets could even incorporate
humour into their political poetry, something that appealed to me.
Humour is an important means by which the human race copes
with being alive, yet humour often gets lost when North American
writers approach "serious" subjects. Not so with, for example,
Eastern European poets or these guerrillas. The following poem is
by a Nicaraguan Sandinista poet, Leonel Rugama, shot by the army
in 1970 after a firefight in Managua lasting several hours. Ruguma
was twenty years old. His poem "The Earth Is a Satellite of the
Moon," is also translated by Margaret Randall.

The apollo 2 cost more than the apollo 1
the apollo 1 cost enough.

The apollo 3 cost more than the apollo 2
the apollo 2 cost more than the apollo 1
the apollo 1 cost enough.

The apollo 4 cost more than the apollo 3
the apollo 3 cost more than the apollo 2
the apollo 2 cost more than the apollo 1
the apollo 1 cost enough.

The apollo 8 cost a whole lot but you didn't feel it
because the astronauts were protestants
they read the bible from the moon,
bringing glad tidings to all christians
and Pope Paul VI blessed them when they
    returned.

The apollo 9 cost more than all the rest together
including the apollo 1 which cost enough.

The great-grandparents of the people of Acahualinca
    were less hungry than the grandparents.
The great-grandparents died of hunger.

The grandparents of the people of Acahualinca
    were less hungry than the parents.
The grandparents died of hunger.

The parents of the people of Acahualinca were
    less hungry than the people who live there now.
The parents died of hunger.

The people of Acahualinca are less hungry than
    their children.
The children of the people of Acahualinca are
    born dead from hunger,
and they're hungry at birth, to die of hunger.

The people of Acahualinca die of hunger.

Blessed be the poor, for they shall inherit the moon.

I must add that part of the fascination of the guerrilla poems for me was the belief that events in the U.S. were moving towards a moment when those of us opposed to the government might be compelled ourselves to take up arms. The same moral force that led us to try to stop the U.S. part in the Vietnam War made it difficult for us to settle for ineffective protest when what was clearly needed was a restructuring of U.S. society to benefit more of the population at home and to end military intervention around the world. And we knew from the armed response to black struggles in the ghettos of Watts, Detroit, and elsewhere that the U.S. government would not hesitate to use guns against its own people engaged in activities that *truly* threatened the status quo.

I tried to capture in a poem written about this time, "The Dream of the Guerrillas," the feeling of being morally pressured towards an escalation of our struggle. The poem appeared in my first collection, *Waiting for Wayman*, published in 1973.

> *With their heavy boots, with their old rifles,*
> *with the clear morning of the world in their hands,*
> *the guerrilleros arrive.*
> *The guerrilleros arrive and they bring the dawn.*
>
> — Felix Pita Rodriguez

In the night, in the lonely bed
the dream of the guerrillas:
hillsides of vast carnival structures
of steel, whirling me out to a lost handgrip
after my father waits with one leg in
my brother's coffin, whirling,
as a stream of lead hoses a body to bits
under the noise of the nightly warplanes.

The tangle of sheets in itchy skin.
The first guitar notes from
under the floor, with the creak of leather
and the feel of gun oil on their fingers, sweat
under the broad sun, and laughing the windy hair
from their eyes, they stand up;
they are the only men of the age who can stand
kneed in the back, gasping in water,
shot into spasms at short range
they rise, open their books to a clean page
and begin. And of the coolness of her body:
freeways turn in the dark, spinning
a string of lights past huge signs and music
saying: the guerrillas, the guerrillas are coming
for you, and you must go with them.

And night quiet
after the dream.
Street lights burn on.
The slogans are calm on dim walls. The clock,
the clock says: now
the guerrillas are coming and you must go with them.

The third of the four threads that constituted political poetry for
me was the knowledge that the head of the Vietnamese struggle,
Ho Chi Minh, was himself a poet. So was the leader of revolutionary
China, Mao Tse-tung. The concept that these leaders not only had
moral right on their side, but also were poets, was tremendously
important to me.

The poetry of Ho and Mao gave status to an art form that in
North America is looked on with great suspicion, if not distaste, by
the population at large. Ho and Mao were leaders who had helped
end the rule by colonial powers and dictatorships of the rich in their
countries, and who actively opposed U.S. support for corrupt and
brutal regimes many places around the globe. Yet, in addition, these
leaders were proud of writing *poems!* The differences from official

North American attitudes to both foreign policy and poetry were heady ones to contemplate.

"Fine Weather" is a poem by Ho that came to us in an era when B-52s were dropping tons of bombs daily on a poor country that nevertheless was successfully resisting at a staggering cost U.S. attempts to inflict its will on the people there. I never knew who the translator was, but for some years I had Ho's poem posted on my wall:

> The wheel of the law turns
> without pause.
>
> After the rain, good weather.
> In the wink of an eye
>
> The universe throws off
> its muddy clothes.
>
> For ten thousand miles
> the landscape
>
> spreads out like a beautiful brocade.
> Light breezes. Smiling flowers.
>
> High in the trees, amongst
> the sparkling leaves
>
> all the birds sing at once.
> Men and animals rise up reborn.
>
> What could be more natural?
> After sorrow, comes joy.

From the tone of quiet assurance expressed in Ho's poem, it was easy to be confident that Vietnam would win, that the victory of right over evil would be as natural as a change of season.

Besides being a poet, Mao Tse-tung expressed literary ideas that were quite important to my developing attitudes towards writing. In the Chinese leader's *Talks at the Yenan Forum on Literature and Art,* Mao asks writers and artists to consider who their art is being created *for.* This question remains vital to me, since the way writers are trained or the way writers respond to the existing literary world contains many hidden assumptions about who the audience for contemporary poetry is or ever could be. And it is only a step from thinking about who you write for, to thinking about *why* you want to write: what is your *purpose* in being a writer? I find these issues excellent ones to put before advanced writing students when I teach, since the students' answers often expose many unexamined ideas about the nature and aim of imaginative writing, and about the society into which that writing will pass when published.

Mao also suggests that the concept of political poetry can be expanded to include *all* poetry. "In the world today," Mao says in his Yenan talks, "all culture, all literature and art belong to definite classes and are geared to definite political lines. There is in fact no such thing as art for art's sake, art that stands above classes or art that is detached from or independent of politics." By this argument, any poem can be regarded as political, as much for what it omits as for what it includes. This latter idea was expressed by the German playwright Bertolt Brecht in his poem "To Posterity" (from the translation by H. R. Hays): "Ah, what an age it is / When to speak of trees is almost a crime / For it is a kind of silence about injustice!" I still like this concept, since I believe there is a hidden politics in the topics literature is silent about, as well as the topics literature expresses.

I have stated elsewhere my belief that what we choose to write about, and select to teach in our schools as literature, conveys a system of values. The women's movement showed us that if in our writing and teaching we omit an accurate account of the experiences of women, we are saying that these experiences have no value. Similarly I have argued that if in our writing and teaching we omit an accurate account of the experiences of daily work, we are saying that these experiences have no value. Such statements, even when made by omission, are *political* statements. For example, every anthology of Canadian or American literature presents by inference a *portrait* of these societies. Each time I pick up another such anthology that largely or entirely omits the experiences of women, and/or of people of colour, and/or of daily work, I believe a *political* choice has been made by the editors, whether consciously or unconsciously.

Also, as a corollary to these ideas, the women's movement has articulated the idea that "the *personal* is political." How someone behaves in their personal life is a better indication of that man's or woman's actual politics than what causes they claim to espouse. Similarly, attitudes revealed by the author in a poem on any subject, no matter how apparently intimate, can indicate the politics of the poet as clearly as what he or she may write in a poem on an overtly political subject. The U.S. author Marge Piercy puts the argument this way in her poem "In the Men's Room(s)":

> I get coarse when the abstract nouns start flashing.
> I go out to the kitchen to talk cabbages and habits.
> I try hard to remember to watch what people do.
> Yes, keep your eyes on the hands, let the voice go
>   buzzing.
> Economy is the bone, politics is the flesh,
> watch who they beat and who they eat,
> watch who they relieve themselves on, watch who
>   they own.
> The rest is decoration.

These ideas, as mentioned above, permit *every* poem to be discussed as political. However I am limiting my discussion here to my response to imaginative writing that because of its *content*, its evident considerations of social questions, is conventionally regarded as political poetry. And the fourth and final thread that helped to form my initial sense of this writing was poems that deal directly with past and contemporary social struggles in North America.

One of the reasons many of us who were activists in the 1960s turned to events, organizations, and personalities in the Third World for inspiration was that we had been cut off from meaningful awareness of the labour and other social movements that had taken place before our time on this continent. The fears created by McCarthyism in the 1950s had resulted in a vast public silence being wrapped around the movements for change that had occurred in our society thirty, forty, fifty years before. As a result, people who had experiences and knowledge from these movements did not pass on to us what they had so painfully learned; in much North American activism we were forced to reinvent the wheel.

I recall my excitement at discovering the political writings of the poet Kenneth Rexroth, who had been active in the twenties and thirties in Chicago, San Francisco, and many other places across the U.S. I remember sitting in the stacks of the library of Colorado State University, where I had gone to teach in 1968, reading Rexroth's poem "For Eli Jacobson" with an activist friend. For the first time I had a real sense that others before us had trod the path we were on. The poem, an elegy, showed that although the people who had gone ahead had not been successful, they had relished the journey — just as we already comprehended, I think, that these brief years would be among the highlights of our lives.

December, 1952

There are few of us now, soon
There will be none. We were comrades
Together, we believed we
Would see with our own eyes the new
World where man was no longer
Wolf to man, but men and women
Were all brothers and lovers
Together. We will not see it.
We will not see it, none of us.
It is farther off than we thought.
In our young days we believed

That as we grew old and fell
Out of rank, new recruits, young
And with the widsom of youth,
Would take our places and they
Surely would grow old in the
Golden Age. They have not come.
They will not come. There are not
Many of us left. Once we
Marched in closed ranks, today each
Of us fights off the enemy,
A lonely isolated guerrilla.
All this has happened before,
Many times. It does not matter.
We were comrades together.
 Life was good for us. It is
Good to be brave — nothing is
Better. Food tastes better. Wine
Is more brilliant. Girls are more
Beautiful. The sky is bluer
For the brave — for the brave and
Happy comrades and for the
Lonely brave retreating warriors.
You had a good life. Even all
Its sorrow and defeats and
Disillusionments were good,
Met with courage and a gay heart.
You are gone and we are that
Much more alone. We are one fewer,
Soon we shall be none. We know now
We have failed for a long time.
And we do not care. We few will
Remember as long as we can,
Our children may remember,
Some day the world will remember.
Then they will say, "They lived in

The days of the good comrades.
It must have been wonderful
To have been alive then, though it
Is very beautiful now."
We will be remembered, all
Of us, always, by all men,
In the good days now so far away.
If the good days never come,
We will not know. We will not care.
Our lives were the best. We were the
Happiest men alive in our day.

I also admired the way Rexroth incorporates a love of the North American wilderness with his concerns for social justice. Like many people in the U.S. and Canada, getting out into the woods was something we enjoyed. Yet justifying such pleasures in the face of the ongoing and urgent demands of the social movements we were involved with was always a problem. Rexroth could close this gap with astonishing ease. A favourite example of mine that illustrates this ability of Rexroth's is "The Great Nebula of Andromeda." This poem is a section of a longer work called "The Lights in the Sky Are Stars," dedicated to his daughter Mary.

We get into camp after
Dark, high on an open ridge
Looking out over five thousand
Feet of mountains and mile
Beyond mile of valley and sea.
In the star-filled dark we cook
Our macaroni and eat
By lantern light. Stars cluster
Around our table like fireflies.
After supper we go straight
To bed. The night is windy
And clear. The moon is three days

Short of full. We lie in bed
And watch the stars and the turning
Moon through our little telescope.
Late at night the horses stumble
Around camp and I awake.
I lie on my elbow watching
Your beautiful sleeping face
Like a jewel in the moonlight.
If you are lucky and the
Nations let you, you will live
Far into the twenty-first
Century. I pick up the glass
And watch the Great Nebula
Of Andromeda swim like
A phosphorescent amoeba
Slowly around the Pole. Far
Away in distant cities
Fat-hearted men are planning
To murder you while you sleep.

Besides discovering a few activist writers from the past, like Rexroth, we read the poets published in current movement journals and newspapers who tackled matters that arose out of activism in our own time. To me the U.S. poetry anthology from the era that best conveys this content, combined with a high level of artistic skill, is *The Whites of Their Eyes,* edited by Paul Hunter, Patti Parson, and Tom Parson. The anthology was a double issue of Seattle's *Consumption* magazine in 1970.

On the back of *The Whites of Their Eyes* the editors reprint a quote from Che Guevara, stating that a guerrilla's pack "must contain . . . only essential items." A vertical dotted line stretches down the centre of the back cover of the paperback anthology and the editors observe:

This book may be folded on the dotted line and carried in the hip pocket. If by poor planning or accident you are caught without it, you're on your own. Poems can be carried in the head, for emergencies.

And in order to emphasize that poetry is no less essential to the struggle than anything else, the anthology contains more than poems from the antiwar, Black, Native American, Chicano, and women's movements. Also included are sections giving advice on coping with arrest and with the different types of tear gas used by U.S. authorities in those days (CS, CN, Nausea and Blister gases, and Mace). There is information on how to bring down police helicopters (nylon kite strings) and, my favourite, a rhymed tip on postering: "Canned milk makes about the best wall poster glue around. Wet the back, smooth it flat, in 20 minutes it won't scrape down."

The Whites of Their Eyes is where I first encountered Diane di Prima's long poem "Revolutionary Letters." With great bravery she tackles, among other issues, an important contradiction that still plagues movements for social change. While the poor of this world quite justifiably want more of what the rich have, some citizens of richer societies are now aware that the ecological cost of these possessions is too great. Here is section 34 of "Revolutionary Letters." Di Prima employs a jargon term of the era, "chicks," to refer to women. The women's movement was beginning to oppose strongly this kind of language back then.

> hey man let's make a revolution, let's give
> every man a thunderbird
> color TV, a refrigerator, free
> antibiotics, let's build
> apartments with a separate bedroom for every child
> inflatable plastic sofas, vitamin pills
> with all our daily requirements that come in the mail
> free gas & electric & telephone &
> no rent. why not?
>
> hey man, let's make a revolution, let's
> turn off the power, turn on the

stars at night, put metal
back in the earth, or at least not take it out
anymore, make lots of guitars and flutes, teach
   the chicks
how to heal with herbs, let's learn
to live with each other in a smaller space, and build
hogans, and domes and teepees all over the place
BLOW UP THE PETROLEUM LINES, make the cars
into flower pots or sculptures or live
in the bigger ones, why not?

In another section she cautions people not to regard acquisition of the products of a consumer society as the sole method of attaining happiness: "remember / you can have what you ask for, ask for / everything."

Former SDS head Todd Gitlin, in another poem ("Who Are the People?") in *The Whites of Their Eyes,* warns against the moral smugness that some activists display. Such smugness is in part due to the righteousness of the activists' cause combined with their minority position in society. The setting for his lesson is a demonstration confronted by police:

i

There are words a man will not speak to your face
but only at a distance
amplified into the State
a clatter of tin:
"In the name of the people
of the State of California

                              "We are the people!"

I order you to disperse"

                              "We are the people!"
                              jabbing our fists in
                                 the air
                              less awkwardly than
                                 we used to

Having long ago dispersed
from the valley home of our sources
we are only now looking to come together again
And who can forget the first time
he visioned the people
marching through his mouth?

    ii

"We are the people!"
Proud words
rattling around in a closed circle
Pride in a closed circle
sounds like bragging
after a while:
"My 'people'
can beat the shit
out of your 'people'"
Watch out for the ricochet,
the nonpeople scratching their heads
with their fists

If we are the people
then how long does the served-out waitress wait?
the secret secretary typing for the people?
the janitor sweeping up after the people?
those who buy lies in a seller's market
licking the chops they think are theirs?

"They don't understand"
Teach
"They won't learn"
You learn more,
then teach
Show how separate fingers become a fist
but the fist is still made up of fingers

Show that anyone may recognize himself
in you

iii

"We shall be the people"
Now you're talking

The waitress, secretary, and janitor who in Todd Gitlin's poem are "nonpeople" as far as some activists are concerned were responsible in large measure for the change I underwent after the 1960s in how I regard politics. Once the pace of activity against the war began to slow, a number of problems with the worldview I held in those days became evident to me. These difficulties especially, but not entirely, were concerned with the status of work and the working life in society and literature. Such problems, and the transformation in my perception of politics that resulted, have also altered my sense of what constitutes meaningful political poetry.

Developments both internal and external to the social change movements I took part in during the late 1960s showed me flaws in how I understood the world. I attended the 1969 SDS convention in Chicago as a delegate from Colorado, and so witnessed the process by which an effective radical student organization was destroyed by competing authoritarian sects. Meanwhile the women's movement consistently pointed out that within SDS, as in many so-called libertarian organizations, the denigration and oppression of women was an integral part of how these groups functioned. I came to the point of disagreeing strongly with the sentiment expressed by Brecht in another stanza of his poem "To Posterity": "Alas, we / Who wished to lay the foundations of kindness / Could not ourselves be kind." The women's movement convincingly demonstrated that a hierarchical, patriarchal structure was unlikely to secure for *anybody* the better life it denied to half the human race within its own ranks. I thus had to conclude that those who could not themselves be kind were unlikely to "lay the foundations of kindness" for others.

In the larger world I was troubled by news from within numerous so-called workers' states, whose revolutionary opposition to U.S. intervention in Vietnam and elsewhere had meant so much to me. For example, Cuba in 1971 passed its Law on Loafing, a kind of national conscription for work that declared being without a job was a crime. It even included a "precriminal state of loafing" for people who had finished school but had not yet held a first job. I was dismayed to read eventually the Chinese trade union law, which forbade any workers' organizations existing outside the approval of the ruling party. And since I have friends employed as tugboat and fishboat deckhands, I became upset by the often repeated Maoist slogan, "Sailing the seas depends on the Helmsman," referring to Mao as the helmsman of China's ship of state. I knew well by this time that sailing the seas, like any job, depends on the skills, labour and imagination of *everybody* who works at that task.

As a person who writes and publishes, while also being employed at a variety of jobs, I became acutely aware of the absence of an accurate account of daily work in the imaginative literature of every nation on earth, whether these countries called themselves "Communist" or "democratic" or both. As I spell out in some critical articles eventually collected in my *Inside Job: Essays on the New Work Writing*, published in 1983, I concluded there is an enormous taboo that surrounds an accurate depiction of daily work and working lives. And the reason for this taboo mainly accounts for my present attitudes towards politics and political poetry.

I believe, as I say in *Inside Job*, that this taboo exists because we are not free at work. Literature, or any other art, that breaks this taboo and accurately portrays everyday work presents the real political situation of the inhabitants of a country. Here is how the U.S. social critic Bob Black presents the case:

> The official line in the U.S. and Canada is that we all have rights and live in a democracy. Those unfortunates who aren't free like us live in police states. They obey orders no matter how arbitrary. The authorities keep them under regular surveillance. State bureaucrats control even the smallest details of

everyday life. Dissent and disobedience are punished. Inform-
ers report regularly to the authorities. All this is supposed to
be a very bad thing.

And so it is, although it is nothing but a description of the
modern workplace. The liberals and conservatives and libertar-
ians who attack totalitarianism are all phonies and hypocrites.
There is more freedom in any moderately de-Stalinized dictatorship than there is in the ordinary American workplace. . . .

A worker is a part-time slave. The boss says when to show up,
when to leave, and what to do in the meantime. He tells you
how much work to do and how fast. He is free to carry his
control to humiliating extremes, regulating, if he so desires,
the clothes you wear or how often you can go to the bathroom.
With a few exceptions he can fire you for any reason, or no
reason. He spies on you by means of snitches and supervisors;
he amasses a dossier on you. If you talk back you are accused
of insubordination, just as if you were a naughty child.

This demeaning system rules at least half the waking hours of a
majority of men and women for most of their lives. Anybody who
says these people are "free" is lying or stupid. . . . People who are
regimented all their lives are psychologically enslaved. Their
aptitude for autonomy is so atrophied that they develop an acute
fear of freedom. The obedience training at their jobs carries over
into the families they start, thus reproducing the system.

I now see politics as authoritarian versus anti-authoritarian
rather than in terms of left versus right. And, for me, the real test
of the presence of democracy is what everyday work is like in a
country, community, or organization. I find this test more useful as
a means of analyzing what occurs in the world than some of my
former ideas. Otherwise how could I explain the odd coincidence
that both a "right-wing" political group like B.C.'s Social Credit
Party and a "left-wing" political group like, say, any former East

European Communist Party, propose *identical* programmes for labour? Both, if you scrape the rhetoric off what they say, want all strikes
banned on pain of jail or worse, and want unions to be either
powerless or at the very least regulated by the government in order
to exist.

No political party or government in the world wants democracy
extended to the workplace. I have come to regard this fact as basic
to the politics of our era, and thus basic to the political *poetry* of our
time. It follows that the new poetry that accurately portrays work is,
in my opinion, the *essence* of political poetry, even when its content
consists solely of revealing some aspect of daily work in our time
and place.

As for poems that describe an *overtly* political content, I now
believe they should share with the new work writing certain characteristics. These characteristics, I am convinced, lead to accuracy and
authenticity, two virtues I want for poetry and which I feel are
essential for any form of social poetry. After all, if we can't see clearly
and precisely where we are as a society, how are we going to figure
out how to get from here to the kind of society we prefer? In *Inside
Job* I explain how the new work writing is distinguished by looking
at work with an *insider's* eye, rather than the eye of an outsider,
however sympathetic. Only in this way is an *accurate* depiction of the
situation possible, since even a sympathetic outsider can miss what
it *feels* like to be personally involved in a given situation or event.
And, as a consequence of that insider's eye, the new work writing
expresses a wealth of detail, detail that in many cases *only* an insider
could know. This detail makes tangible for a reader the authenticity
of the lives described.

Finally, in the new work writing, there is considerable use of
humour, which to me reproduces a true and vital means by which
the human race responds to difficulties. As I explain in *Inside Job,*
only an insider knows what is *unusual* about a certain workplace
situation or event, and therefore what is a potential source of
humour. To an outsider things almost always look deadly serious.

Translating these characteristics to political poetry as the term is
ordinarily understood, I now find I have little patience for an

outsider's political poem no matter how successful artistically. Someone who writes a moving response to something they read about in a newspaper or pamphlet is likely responding to inaccuracy, to exaggeration, to only part of the story. I now demand of my political poets that either they participate in social movements here in North America, or have some firsthand experience of what they are describing, or link through some means what they are talking about to their own lives. I want to see *details* that reveal the poet is closer to the situation than having watched some five- or ten-second news clip on television. And I want these poems occasionally to display the *humour* that also demonstrates the writer is inside an aspect of the situation, however terrible, the poem depicts.

One instance in my own writing of where I had to meet the challenge of my new criteria for political poetry occurred in 1973. In September of that year the elected government of Salvador Allende in Chile was overthrown by the military because of Allende's attempts to introduce certain new social programmes, just as in 1981 the military would declare war on the Polish people for their experimentation with social reforms. At the time of the 1973 coup I was working assembling hoods in a Burnaby truck manufacturing plant and tried to link events I could only read about with the lives of my friends at work. The following poem, "Larry Tetlock," is one of a series under the title "The Chilean Elegies" that were collected in my third book, *Money and Rain*, published in 1975:

> And where it says *they shot so many factory workers*
> does it mean Larry Tetlock
> who began at this factory three months before me
> after the usual adventures working for Sears
> hanging drapes: trying to install new white ones
> with a spiral screwdriver someone had loaded with oil
> and having his van catch on fire
> from a faulty battery one day while making deliveries?
>
> Is this who they mean? Larry, at 20,
> with a brand new Vega to drive and working

to pay for it, intending to look for another job
if we strike, fed up with the din of this one?

Or is it Ernie they killed? Ernie, who jumped
from the Hungarian Army in '56, learned English
and used to work at General Paint?
Thirty-six and divorced, he was back to Hungary twice
and realizing he would work at the same place
    here or there
elected to stay with racetracks, stereos, and all the
    movies he can see?
"I'm always happy," Ernie says one day
when everybody is angry at him for being so dense.
"I never get depressed. No." Why do they want
to put an end to his jazz collection, his nights
in the Ritz Hotel beer parlor?

But these aren't the men who have died.
These will be back at work Monday, and Tuesday,
    and also Friday
firing Huck bolts and lifting their end of the fender
until they quit and get another job
or until I quit and sit in a room writing lines
until I too get another job. Not Vancouver, but in
    Santiago
in those rainy graveyards surrounded by old houses
partitioned into suites, family areas, and rented rooms
fresh earth is dug, and a sound of crying
a shriek, and a heavy silence goes on
for entire avenues, so many people put into the
    ground
like fill for some seedy construction project
involving the mayor, his uncle the contractor, and
    the pay-off
of a number of zoning officials and building
    inspectors.

Except that it's death. What do they think a man
   understands
who works in these places, a man only the newspapers
and certain theoreticians of the Left consider "a
   factory worker"
a man who believes himself simply to be his own name
   — Larry Tetlock, for instance? Why does an
   order go out for his death?

What if the first thing he knows about bullets
except for a friend who has offered to take him hunting
is the bullet inside his own head that the Army intends
to let him keep forever? What do they think he sees
that they want to sever the optic nerve
so what the eyes take in will never get to the brain
and from there to his hands?

Why cause this disruption in production:
no end of trouble and re-scheduling for
foremen and chargehands, not to mention whole
   families?

Why should they kill Larry Tetlock?

In some of my other explicitly political poems I have attempted
to incorporate humour. But whatever artistic strategy I select, I
continue to believe political poetry is a vital part of poetry. I think
the tasks political poetry can accomplish are worthy ones: to articulate the conscience of society, as well as to provide an accurate
portrayal of aspects of our common life. By means of an insider's
eye, detail, and humour, the best political poetry not only can show
the actual situation we are in, but also can suggest better possibilities
than the official versions of a new, improved existence currently
promoted by the hierarchies of both East and West.

So political poetry can be an inspiration as well as a documentary
or a denunciation. One of my touchstones of this kind of writing is

"On Headaches" by Roque Dalton, a guerrilla poet from El Salvador. I find this poem both instructive and poignant. Although it incorporates comedy and an accurate glimpse at how difficult fundamental social change is to achieve, the poem presents communism as representing the hopes of humanity. Dalton was a founder of El Salvador's People's Revolutionary Army, but he was killed in the underground in El Salvador in 1975 by a faction of his *own* organization. This biographical information makes "On Headaches" not only a funny call to reorganize human life in a better way, but also a stern warning that there are problems and perils with every approach to solving our troubles — and especially with an authoritarian approach. Nevertheless, I love how the poet tries to make evident just how good a bright future might feel. The translation is by Margaret Randall.

> It's beautiful to be a communist
> even though it gives you lots of headaches.
>
> And the thing is that the communist's headaches
> are supposed to be historical, that is to say
> they don't go away with aspirins
> but only with the realization of Paradise on Earth.
> That's how it is.
>
> Under capitalism our heads ache
> and they decapitate us.
> In the struggle for the revolution the head
> is a time-bomb.
>
> In the construction of socialism
> we plan headaches
> which doesn't make them any less frequent, just
> the other way around.
>
> Communism will be, among other things,
> an aspirin the size of the sun.

I am dazzled by that image of the enormous aspirin for the achievement of heaven on earth, even if to me the poet's conception of how to attain this heaven has proven in practice to cause *pain* of stellar proportions. Yet this poem and this poet's history remind us that we must make social change out of our real selves, with all our mental, emotional, and bodily imperfections as well as our strengths. We have to make the effort with our headaches as well as with our moments of joy. Of course, the human race will make mistakes on the road to Paradise — costly and horrible errors as well as silly and laughable ones. I believe the poetry that accompanies our striving for a brighter day for all humanity, as well as for the planet that is our home, must be — among other things — a constant reminder that we *are* human, that social change is about *people*, about improving people's lives — real people's lives: Larry Tetlock's, for instance, and that of the astute and angry speaker in Marge Piercy's poem, and your life and mine. The struggle for a better existence will take many shapes and forms, and at times is very close when we think it is far away. I will conclude with "Teething," a poem about a friend of mine, from my collection, *Living on the Ground*, published in 1980:

> In the dark house, the cry of a child.
> Her teeth are trying to be born:
> the tiny incisors
> are cutting their way up
> through flesh, into a mouth
> now open and crying.
>
> Deep snow around the house
> beside the forest. Indoors, in the night
> the sleepy voice of the mother, then the father,
> and the child's steady crying.
> All at once the father is up, and a moment later
> he brings the child into another room
> and sits in an old rocker.

The noise of the chair starts
as its wooden dowels and slats
adjust repeatedly to the weight being swung
back and forth. The chair moves
not with the easy pace
of someone assured, experienced,
but with the urgent drive of a young man
rocking and rocking. The chair creaks
persistently, determinedly,
like the sound of boots on the snowy road outside
in the day, going somewhere.

                                                But it is here
the father has come to. In the dark room, in the chair
ten years as an adult pass, the chair
rocks out a decade of meetings, organizations, sit-ins.
It rocks out Chicago, and Cook County Jail.
It rocks out any means necessary
to end the War, fight racism, abolish the draft.
It rocks out grad school and marriage.
It rocks out Cambodia, and at last
jobs, a new country, and a child.

                                                But the chair
falls back each time
to the centre of things, so it also rocks back
all these lives up into these lives: the father
rocking
with his child in his arms
at the edge of sleep. In the still house at Salmon Arm
the sound of the rocking chair
in the winter night. Sudden cry of the child.
Cry of the world.

7 VISIBLE CONSEQUENCES, INVISIBLE JOBS: INTRODUCTION TO *PAPERWORK*

We live in a society that hides from itself the basis of its existence. North American culture — high and low, popular or elitist — presents almost nowhere the realities of daily work. Thus, this anthology of poems is a light turned on what our society wraps in darkness: the humour, sadness, joy, anger, and all the other emotions that accompany our participation in the work force.

Our jobs form the central and governing core of our lives. Our daily work — be it blue or white collar, paid or unpaid — determines or strongly influences our standard of living, who our friends are, how much time and energy we have left to spend off the job. Our employment determines or strongly influences where we live and what our attitudes are to an enormous range of events, people, objects, environments. No other activity in daily life has more personal consequences for us than the work we do (or are looking for).

Our jobs also re-create each day every aspect of our society. Because we go to work our fellow citizens are provided with food, shelter, and clothing. Through our employment people are educated and entertained, methods of transportion are organized, children are raised, and much, much more. But an accurate depiction of what occurs in the work force is overlooked and ignored by virtually every aspect of the surrounding culture. An honest examination of daily work is missing from our movies and television, news media, schools, advertising, fine arts.

Something considered taboo must be happening at the centre of our life — and so at the heart of our society — if we are willing to depict endlessly the *consequences* of our jobs, but not to portray the jobs themselves. For example, our literature in book after book, anthology after anthology, presents a literary portrait of a nation, a society, in which *nobody works*. One possible origin for this strange fact is that during twelve years of public education almost no time is devoted to an accurate account of the history and present conditions of employment in North America. What happens to human beings on the job is not considered a topic for major consideration by our school curricula, even though working is the activity that eventually will occupy most of the waking lives of every student.

For instance, as *Paperwork* was in preparation in the fall of 1989, I was sent two new literature textbooks aimed at high schools. Both were organized thematically. One, *Themes on the Journey* (Nelson), identifies what its editor considers the sixteen major themes of "the human journey." These themes include love, death, nature, as well as art, national identity, war. Work is never mentioned. The second collection, *Themes for All Times* (Jesperson Press), identifies seven themes as representing human life "for all times": relationships, faith and belief, conflict, survival, freedom and equality, dealing with today, facing tomorrow. Again nowhere in this text is daily work seen as worthy of mention, let alone study.

This almost *pathological* avoidance of looking at everyday jobs is just as evident in popular culture. Any trip around the TV dial will reveal a complete absence of anything resembling true depictions of daily employment. Where jobs are shown, such as hospital work or police work, the portrayals are fantasies, romanticizations, trivializations. Police work is not like *Hill Street Blues* or *Miami Vice*, any more than medical employment is like *General Hospital* or *St. Elsewhere*. This can be verified by even a few minutes of conversation with an actual nurse, doctor, lawyer, detective, or uniformed officer.

We expect less than honesty from advertising, and we are not disappointed in our expectations when the *source* of advertised products is supposedly presented. My favourite is "The Land of

Dairy Queen," the apparent origin of the tasty ice-cream snacks. Here images of mounds of chocolate and ice cream obscure entirely the realities of cocoa production in the Third World and minimum wage service jobs here at home. How much more pleasant to imagine a magical origin for the objects sold to us than to see clearly where things come from.

Avoiding a consciousness of how human beings really spend their lives is not just an interesting sociological or artistic observation, though. The pervasive taboo against a portrayal of our daily work tangibly *hurts* us.

As a college teacher, I ask my students how many of them, before they selected their course of studies, talked at length to someone doing the job that is the student's career goal. Often half or more of my students have never made this effort. The taboo against an accurate look at daily work has thus put them in some peril: they are expending considerable time, money, and effort preparing themselves for a job about which they have only the shakiest or most romantic impression. More immediately, our high school students graduate, or they drop out, largely ignorant of what labour laws and regulations protect them in the work force, and what opportunities and shortcomings are offered by unemployment insurance, workers' compensation, and similar work-related programmes. Again the potential for pain is great. Young people can fall prey to unscrupulous employers by accepting wages, conditions, and hours that violate legal standards. Or, where young employees sense that laws are being broken, they are uncertain how to seek redress.

Whether we are young or old the taboo hurts us by the cultural silence in which it smothers what happens to us every day on the job. In this eerie quiet each of us feels isolated, uncertain whether we are the only person who responds to our employment as we do. We counter this isolation with shoptalk, gossip about our specific workplace with our immediate peers. But, overall, the silence helps keep us from a collective discussion and understanding of the effects our work has on us, and how we might together fundamentally improve our working lives.

As well, the taboo ensures that our culture perceives our contribution to society as insignificant, for the culture of any society establishes a system of values. What is talked about or otherwise portrayed in art, education, and entertainment is seen as having value. What a society is silent about is implicitly understood to be without importance or merit. As long as the supermarket tabloids suggest we worry about the state of Burt and Loni's relationship rather than consider, say, alternate means of organizing our own daily lives, we are likely to regard ourselves and what happens to us as less important than those figures and events the surrounding culture insists repeatedly are worthy of our attention and concern. For instance, the deaths of seven astronauts are viewed as an international tragedy, and so they are. But why are the deaths of seven miners in a cave-in any less a tragedy? Do not the miners also leave behind spouses, children, unfulfilled hopes and dreams? Why are some individuals so overvalued and the contribution of the majority of us so undervalued?

This situation saps our willingness to act to change our lives for the better. After all, if we are not the important men and women in society, if our contribution to the community is culturally regarded as worthless, why should we speak out or act collectively to improve our lives? And this lack of self-confidence hurts us because it strikes at the root of democracy. As the social critic Bob Black puts it, "Once you drain the vitality from people at work, they'll likely submit to hierarchy in politics, culture, and everything else."

The poems of this collection, although they were written individually for many different reasons, together break the taboo against a depiction of our real lives and affirm the vital importance of what the majority of us do all day. Using humour, wit, outrage, poignancy, and sorrow, the poems celebrate how our work contributes to creating the society in which we all live and how our jobs shape our individual lives. If film stars, sports idols, and politicians were to vanish tomorrow, the world would still be fed, clothed, housed, and so on because of *our* efforts. This is not the message that bombards us daily from TV screens, billboards, books, magazines, art exhibits, and classrooms. But *Paperwork* proves this truth beyond doubt.

The poems of *Paperwork*, however, are not intended to be an exhaustive or comprehensive look at the new work writing that has begun to appear in many places across North America. Instead, like its predecessor anthology *Going for Coffee* (Madeira Park, B.C.: Harbour Publishing, 1981), *Paperwork* offers a sampling of what I consider to be the best of the new poetry about jobs and the working life. As with any anthology, then, the selection reflects the strengths and weaknesses of its editor's judgement. My major criterion for including a poem in *Paperwork* — besides literary accomplishment — is that the poem should present an *insider's* view of the workplace. I am convinced that an outsider's vision of a job site or other work situation, however sympathetic, lacks the accuracy that the insider brings to the writing. And accuracy is essential to clear thinking, and writing, about daily employment and its human consequences.

Because *Paperwork* shows us jobs with an insider's eye, we find here both extensive use of detail (often detail only an insider could know) and comedy (since jokes remain a major way the human race gains perspective about its difficulties). A further examination of these and many other facets of the emerging work literature can be found in my *Inside Job: Essays on the New Work Writing* (Harbour, 1983).

The poems in *Paperwork* are grouped into eight sections. "Corn-cobs on the Slag Road" gathers poems concerned with outdoor work; "Something They Claim Can't Be Made" presents poems on women in the paid work force; "Piece by Piece You Deliver Yourself" offers poems on service work; and the fourth section, "The Work of Looking for Work," deals with unemployment.

"Dear Foreman," the fifth section, is about production work indoors, followed by "Calling You on My Break," which contains poems on how jobs affect human relations. The poems of "When They Push the Buttons to Rise" look at work mainly from a managerial perspective, or else describe an employee's direct response to that perspective. The final section, "Less Like Ants," focuses on ways we assess and sometimes resist the limitations our work imposes on us. This section, and *Paperwork*, closes with two poems from the 1983 public sector general strike in B.C. For it is during a general strike, as at no other time, that it becomes absolutely evident that without our work society ceases to function. Not all the words and images of managers or elected officials, nor the fantasies of advertising or entertainment, can define the world during such an event. Our value and importance are unquestioned.

By their very nature, however, poems resist being placed in set categories such as mine here. For example, there are poems about women in paid employment throughout the collection. Assessments of a specific job and/or a working life appear in poems in many sections also. Even my indoor/outdoor distinction is not an exact one: building construction begins outside, for instance, but by the time the last tradespeople are employed, the work is primarily indoors.

So, despite my attempts to slot these poems according to their major topics, this writing insists that it is multidimensional. Exactly like the human beings who wrote the poems, and the men and women about whom they speak, these poems defy any easy generalization and refuse to be narrowly defined. This quality is part of their power as art, and as people. When we look at them, we see as in a mirror our true selves, our real lives. This is not an experience we are used to. We may be exhilarated or depressed, amused or scornful, respectful or enraged at the sight. But until we observe accurately who we are and where we are, we cannot move forward to better our lives. We can shift from one consumer or political fantasy to the next, but that is not the same thing as improving our common existence. It is the gift of these marvellous poems that they show us both our actual present and a door into the future.

8 SPLIT SHIFT AND AFTER: SOME ISSUES OF THE NEW WORK WRITING

Towards the close of the Split Shift Colloquium on the new work writing, held in August 1986 in Vancouver, B.C., a person in the audience summed up the gathering as "a seed, not a flower."

Split Shift, the first North American symposium on contemporary work literature, was a four-day event that brought together about twenty U.S. and Canadian writers, editors, publishers, and educators to give talks and readings and to conduct formal and informal discussions with colloquium audiences as well as one another. And, as a follow-up, the Vancouver work writers' organization that had cosponsored Split Shift assembled nine months later in a sunny East End backyard to further consider five issues raised at the colloquium. Participants at the May 1987 gathering felt that an examination of these topics was necessary to advance an ongoing discussion as to how best to nurture this new poetry, fiction, and drama that strives to present accurately how daily work informs our lives.

The current imaginative writing about daily work is tagged as "new" by practitioners to distinguish it from the often dreary, programmatic material loosely identified as "socialist realism" and associated in many people's minds with the 1930s. The new contemporary work-based literature is characterized by being written by an insider speaking about her or his own workplace experiences rather than by an outsider. As a result, the writing is full of specific detail and humour.

This literature began to appear in North American anthologies and magazines and individual authors' collections about twenty years ago. A few organizations of writers interested in the development of this material have formed on this continent, but the Split Shift Colloquium at Vancouver's Trout Lake Community Centre was the first time many Americans and Canadians active in this field had a chance to meet face-to-face.

The two sponsors of Split Shift (the name comes from the idea that a writer who is employed works a double shift) were the Vancouver Industrial Writers' Union and the Kootenay School of Writing. The latter is a faculty-run nonprofit institution that grew out of the writing programme at David Thompson University Centre in Nelson, B.C. — a four-year postsecondary facility closed by the provincial Social Credit government in 1984. The Vancouver Industrial Writers' Union was formed in 1979 and links about a dozen authors who meet monthly, host an annual reading series, and carry out other activities designed to promote work literature. Such activities include work writing performances at the 1985 Vancouver Folk Music Festival and the production of a series of show cards featuring contemporary work poems displayed in Vancouver's buses during the city's 1986 centennial. VIWU has issued two anthologies of members' work (*Shop Talk* in 1985 and *More Than Our Jobs* in 1991, both published by Pulp Press) and a cassette of insiders' labour songs and poems, also called *Split Shift*, produced in 1989 jointly with the Vancouver folksong group Fraser Union.

At the 1986 colloquium the accuracy with which the new work literature depicts contemporary jobs was shown by the range of attitudes towards employment expressed in the writing of the invited participants. Exactly as is found in most workplaces today, a spectrum of approaches to labour was evident: from people who find all work odious to those who value their job as a major source of feelings of self-worth.

At one end of the spectrum was the U.S. poet Antler, whose books include *Factory* (about his time in a can manufacturing plant in Minneapolis). Antler's attitude may be summed up by the title of his poem "Zero Hour Day, Zero Day Workweek," which represents his goal for the human race. His poem "Workaholics Anonymous" pits the reality of the "work force" against the idea of a "play force":

> People think it's a disgrace not to work,
>   that one is being irresponsible,
> But actually it's those working ecocide jobs
>   who are most irresponsibly irresponsible.
> The problem is not that the economy is faltering
>   but that freedom is faltering.
> Rather than create more jobs
>   why not create more freedom?
> The more we work the less we're free!

Alongside Antler on the spectrum was a contingent from the editorial collective of San Francisco's *Processed World*. This lively magazine, written mainly by office workers from that city's financial district, calls itself "The Magazine With the Bad Attitude." With characteristic humour the editors offer subscribers a Bad Attitude Certificate, suitable for framing.

Processed World is outspoken in its criticisms of the uselessness and harmfulness of many jobs, especially those in the so-called "electronic office." The magazine's pages include fiction and poetry, work autobiography in the form of "Tales of Toil," articles on the deeds and misdeeds of various corporations, self-examination and soul-searching on the part of contributors about their viewpoints on many aspects of consumer and work life, and fascinating and funny graphics.

Next along the spectrum at Split Shift could be placed Vancouver's Sandy Shreve, who stated that she did not like her work on the clerical support staff of a local university. Yet unsatisfactory conditions under which her job must be performed have led her to become active in her union (as reflected in her poems) as a means to battle for change in the workplace. She is also acutely aware of the difficulties facing women in the working world generally.

A notch to one side of Shreve was Howard White, poet, oral historian, and chronicler of B.C. coastal communities, industries, and people. White has worked for many years as a bulldozer driver (most recently he has been in charge of the Pender Harbour landfill) and operates his own publishing company, as well. He unflinchingly documents in his writings what the primary resource jobs of the B.C. coast do to human beings, their families, and the biosphere. At the same time White takes evident pride in the accomplishments of the men and women of the raincoast, particularly their ability to survive and even occasionally prosper despite a destructive work environment.

A similar willingness to take an honest look at work that is hard on people, combined with an expression of pride in the successful completion of tasks that are set, is found in the poems of Oregon carpenter and Split Shift participant Clemens Starck. In the poet's "Slab on Grade" he considers the socially useful job of pouring the concrete floor of a building:

> What could be flatter or more nondescript
> than a concrete slab?
> For years people will walk on it,
> hardly considering that it was put there
> on purpose,
> on a Thursday in August
> by men on their knees.

Just along the spectrum from Starck is the women-into-trades movement, represented at Split Shift by Susan Eisenberg, a journeywoman electrician from Boston. In a poem from her volume *It's a Good Thing I'm Not Macho* Eisenberg speaks of winning acceptance at her trade at last:

> myself   the only "female"
>   and yet
> we find, almost easily, the language
> that is common:
>   — *Get me some 4-inch squares*
>   *with three-quarter k-o's* —
>   — *Need any couplings or connectors?*
>   — *No, but grab some clips and c-clamps*
>   *and some half-inch quarter-twenties.*

Passwords.
— *You know what you're doing in a panel?*
— *Sure.*

Mechanic to mechanic.

Alongside Eisenberg's place on the spectrum could be slotted Kirsten Emmott, a Vancouver doctor active with VIWU. Emmott's area of special interest is obstetrics. Thus, many of her powerful and moving poems focus on the problems and joys of being a woman doctor in a field where her patients are women.

Beside Emmott, and taking a position at the far end of the spectrum from Antler, were writers such as San Francisco's Robert Carson and Winnipeg's Jim McLean. Carson is a founder of the former San Francisco work writers' group, the Waterfront Writers and Artists. This organization consisted of a number of longshoremen and ship's clerks who for some years functioned similarly to VIWU, except that Waterfront Writers were all employed at the same trade and in many cases saw one another daily on the job. Like Carson, many of the former Waterfront writers consider themselves part of a harbour occupational community with a commonly recognized history and set of customs. Many are second- or third-generation dockworkers. Participation in this occupational community is an integral part of their sense of self-worth. Carson is not unique in having returned to the docks after having earned a college degree (in his case, a master's in creative writing).

For McLean, too, his occupation is an important part of his self-definition. McLean apprenticed as a railway carman after high school in Moose Jaw and completed twenty-four years with CP Rail in that trade before being made a safety supervisor. "The railway has been good to me," he told the Split Shift audience. McLean is aware, of course, that others do not share his perception of the company. In his collection of poems *The Secret Life of Railroaders* he lists in one poem some samples of the "bitter verses" he has seen "over and over again, scrawled on the sides of box cars":

> *up hill slow*
> *down hill fast*
> *tonnage first*
> *safety last*

and

> *broken strikes*
> *and broken tools*
> *dirt and death*
> *and books of rules*

McLean writes and talks with great sensitivity to different responses to the work experience. But he is firm in his own beliefs; his talk at Split Shift was entitled "From the Other Side: Writing from the Management Side of the Workplace." McLean's considerable humanity displayed in his talk led Vancouver bus driver Bob Smith to stand in the audience after McLean finished and state he was glad McLean was not a supervisor for B.C. Transit because "I would find it hard to hate *your* guts."

Smith, incidentally, has written about his work in a vein close to that of Antler or *Processed World*'s contributors. Smith once described himself in print as "a retired social worker, a retired steel mill worker, a retired truck painter who wants to be a retired bus driver as soon as possible." In an article on how at age forty he is already looking forward to not working, Smith writes:

> It was fun for a while there, learning how to direct 40-foot vehicles through the eyes of moving needles. But even as you come out of training you are aware you have already spent more time behind the wheel of a bus than you have spent lying on a hill watching the clouds roll by. You have already spent

more time opening doors for passengers than you have spent teaching your kid how to fish.

With sentiments like the above one we have returned to the opposite end of the spectrum from Jim McLean. And indeed it was one of the most exciting aspects of Split Shift to witness people such as Antler and McLean talking one-on-one, exploring the dimensions of each other's views. For although these writers' conclusions about daily work differ greatly, they at least share a common wish to create a literature out of an accurate portrayal of the contemporary working life.

At Split Shift there was wide agreement on some positive aspects to work — whether or not a particular speaker felt these aspects could be better realized some other way than through employment. The beneficial dimensions to work include, besides economic survival, the social interactions found on every job, a sense of contributing to the larger community, and a sense of personal accomplishment.

The colloquium also touched on the question of the audience for work writing: who they are now and what the potential might be. A morning session with three teachers introduced the audience to how work writing is being used now in some high school and adult basic education classrooms. Stephanie Smith, who at the time was the director of the Watsonville project of the California Literacy Campaign, spoke about the use of work writing material in literacy education. She brought along samples of her students' writing, such as the following by José Acosta:

> I don't like working in the fields
> It's hot and it's hard to pick the strawberries
> When I work in the fields
> "Ugh — aye, my back — "
> It's a green sea and a
> Thousand men they bend
> Down and you can't see them
> Anymore — they are part of the sea

> Pain and satisfaction — all mixed
> You have them with you all the time

Yet in spite of the varied topics that were covered during the hectic days and nights of Split Shift, to many people present there seemed an introductory feeling about the colloquium. The newness of the contemporary work writing movement resulted in Split Shift resembling at times more of a "show and tell" session than a writers' meeting where technical or philosophic issues of importance to the artists are debated in-depth. Hence the audience member's characterization of Split Shift as a seed, not a flower. By the close of Split Shift the Vancouver work writers' group had begun to try to assess what problems the colloquium revealed in the work writing movement. In conversation with one another VIWU members eventually isolated five issues they felt Split Shift had not tackled in enough depth. These were discussed at VIWU's later gathering, dubbed After the Shift.

The first issue arises out of a difficulty almost all work writers have encountered. How can sexist, racist, or other antihuman attitudes found in the work force be realistically depicted in a manner so that a reader does not mistake the documentary impulse for an *endorsement* of these ideas? Discussion at After the Shift centred for convenience on two poems by Windsor poet Eugene McNamara, from his book *Call It a Day*. The poems of McNamara's collection chart a novice's introduction to the industrial life of Chicago, a milieu in which McNamara himself began work. Some VIWU members found the two poems in question sexist, while others felt McNamara's *dislike* of the attitudes expressed in the poems led him to write the pieces.

In McNamara's "Lily" the speaker remembers a sixteen-year-old "working / in the office" of his factory with whom he had a relationship:

> even the drivers coming
> in off the routes slam
> their clipboard down
> going through the manifests

> kept it cool; no foul mouth
> she was everybodys sister
> daughter in her little
> girl flat shoes no stockings
> i found no pants in
> back of the stock cabinets
> that summer

The speaker recalls "she was a music student / someplace i forget where" and the poem ends with a muted statement of regret by the speaker for his personal situation: "oh lily / i am older now still here."

The poem "Ruth from Payroll" describes how a woman as part of her job has to walk into a machine shop and suffer the response of the "hunched men" who "look up / from the machines." The speaker portrays the woman as he sees her and also how the other male employees react to her presence:

> she struts through the
> smoked air on high heels from
> another world she has a different
> blouse for every day all frilly
> all tight all boob dance shes
> about forty old gus says them
> older women are best they give
> you that dying quiver she has
> thighs like a shetland she knows
> the eyes are eating her a low
> moan starts up a whistle some
> one says ruthie here it is for
> you a hammer bangs on a bench
> shes made it through the shop
> again without getting raped
> her ass must hurt from all the
> stares hitting it everyday

In discussing these two poems Sandy Shreve said that to her they fail because they are *only* a description of events and attitudes and they need to be more. "You try to portray what happens," she said, "but also try to get *behind* what happens. What's the next lot of feelings? What lies beyond or under the experience? What could be different?"

Even if the speaker in a poem is limited in his or her consciousness, Shreve said, this limitation must be clear to the reader. "Why does the speaker feel this way? What has *led* people to feel this way? What has created these attitudes?" Not to provide such a perspective is a limitation of realism as a technique, Shreve felt, since there is more to the actual situation being documented than just someone regarding another person as an object. As a means to get beyond the one-dimensional depiction of Lily or Ruth, Shreve said, the author could at least describe more about his subject — presenting them as employees, too, for instance.

Glen Downie, a medical social worker, disagreed with Shreve. He emphasized the need to look at the context of the poems. He also stated that a poem often cannot contain all the dimensions to a social problem or event it depicts. "You have to selectively focus on that piece of the reality which you can recognize yourself and portray," he said.

As a positive example of a writer handling a potentially sexist situation, Shreve cited VIWU member Mark Warrior's poem in which the speaker while employed at a logging camp recalls his homelife. In this poem, "Revolt of the Pens," as the speaker waits in a frosty marshaling yard one morning, he remembers certain intimate details of his girlfriend's body. He starts to list these details in the poem, but there is an interruption:

> my pen
> is marching across the page
> with a picket sign, crying
> "enough! this crap
> is boring! lies! enough!"

The speaker then announces that, "in compliance with Article VI, section 2" of his pens' "new contract," he admits that the intimate description he began "is entirely a fabrication" and that what he really remembered in the yard while waiting to go to work "was an afternoon / spent watching you read / the newspaper on the back porch."

Kirsten Emmott reinforced the seriousness of men's harassment of women, on the job or off, by describing her frustration and anger at facing this demeaning treatment year after year. She spoke about once having to cross a city park in the course of her duties. Observing a work crew clearing brush beside the path about the middle of the park, she dreaded subjecting herself to the comments she knew she would have to endure if she walked past the crew.

"I was about thirty years old," Emmott said. "I'd had many years of this already. And I thought: 'Why do I have to do this? Is there some way I can get all the way around the park? But I don't have time. It would take me 20 minutes.' And I walked along the path and when I got there, they were all women. I was just so happy, I was almost in tears. I don't think men have ever realized what we have to go through."

Kate Braid, a carpenter, told of working on a construction project downtown where the men on her job site would whistle and shout comments at women passing on the street. "How do you think she feels?" Braid asked the men working with her. She said she went on: "Do you want her to say hello? And they'd say, 'Uh, oh, sure.' And I'd say, 'Then say hello!'" She herself would smile and speak to the women on the sidewalk and the women would respond in a friendly manner. "The guys would look at me like: 'Wow. How did you do that?'" Braid said.

On the issue of depicting racist attitudes the discussion focused on the problem of dialects. In the workplace, as in Canadian society generally, lack of facility with English is often equated with stupidity. So dialect jokes are a staple of racist humour. Where writers try to counter racist attitudes by depicting the sayings of non-Anglo co-workers, dialect is sometimes employed, too. But the consensus at After the Shift was that dialect constitutes a different language.

Unless the author is raised in, or otherwise is intimately familiar with, that language, dialect is extremely difficult to capture correctly and convincingly — even for the best of purposes.

Overall, since the new work writing is based on the concept that an insider can most accurately depict the experiences of a working life, a work author is left with a dilemma should she or he wish to portray immigrant or other perspectives not the author's own. Yet longer literary forms, like the novel or theatre, demand the presence of characters with important life experiences different from the author's. The people attending After the Shift agreed that the dangers of inaccuracy are considerable when an outsider-author assumes the point of view of such a character.

Brad Barber, who at the time of the gathering worked as a construction labourer, introduced the second issue VIWU wanted to explore: how much should a writer's *vocabulary* reflect an insider's knowledge of an occupation? Because the new work authors are describing jobs from the viewpoint of someone within the work experience, work literature often uses terms familiar only to an insider. For instance, VIA Rail service manager Erin Mouré's poem, "Graig's Talk," includes the lines:

> After working a year wherever they asked,
> finally trained as a waiter and liking it:
> he's force-assigned in the pantry all summer
> tho he didn't bid,
> wanting the big money doubling out spare,
> dreaming of Asia

Here terms from how VIA Rail and its unions organize job assignments ("force-assigned," "bid," "doubling out spare") may not be understood by a reader. But in the context of the poem the precise meaning of the terms is less important than the sense that the character Graig is unhappy with where VIA Rail has placed him.

Barber spoke of how the use of insider's jargon in a poem or story can help place a reader within the world of the occupation being described. As well, the terms sometimes reveal a particular attitude insiders have towards an aspect of their working existence. An off-the-job example is the name motorcycle racers apply to the scraped skin, cuts, and bruises they obtain in falls: "road rash."

Different strategies for coping with jargon in imaginative writing were discussed. Techniques used include the provision of a glossary at the bottom of the page or at the end of the literary work or collection, or the incorporation of an explanation of terms into the poem or story if such a definition can be made unselfconsciously. In Jim McLean's poems about railroading he often provides an introductory prose description that defines the technical terms, just as a poet giving a public reading might introduce a poem with such an explanation.

Use of work jargon can create a sense of mystery about the job, too. The presence of these terms thus teaches outsiders that there is more to this work than they imagined previously. At the same time those who do the job are reminded that, at least in this aspect of their lives, they are the ones "in the know" rather than the officially sanctioned bearers of knowledge like teachers, politicians, corporate "experts," et cetera. Hence such use of jargon can help reinforce an occupational group's sense of itself as a tightly knit crew with pride in its skills and daily achievements.

People at After the Shift also expressed their enjoyment of how the insider's names of tasks and tools provide a certain flavour in a literary work. The use of names from the job can add a taste of the exotic to, or otherwise enrich, the vocabulary of a poem, story, or play. Kate Braid mentioned a poem from a women-into-trades magazine that consists entirely of the names of tools.

The third issue of the five discussed at After the Shift was concerned with how a writer's choice of vocabulary and artistic form reveals a hidden audience for his or her writing. The level of sophistication of vocabulary and of figures of speech used by an author show that, consciously or unconsciously, the writer is aiming her or his writing at a particular class or group. Similarly a decision to write in the form of modern poetry — as much of the new work writing does — implies a severe limitation on the potential audience for the literary piece.

Howard White described the problem for work writers, and his own solution, as part of a "Statement of Purpose" prepared for the Split Shift Colloquium:

> It would be interesting to ask most work poets who they have in mind when they write: the lunch room bunch, or the editors and reviewers of *Event, Going for Coffee, Minnesota Review.* I don't know what most would say. It would be interesting. If you asked me I would say they have to be thinking of the other writers because, like my own poems, their poems almost exclusively use the syntax of modern poetry, a special codified syntax which is known only to students of contemporary literature, and is unlike ordinary speech and unlike traditional poetry and has a perplexing effect on most working people.
>
> And along with this specialized syntax goes a specialized imaginative environment that is not the environment of the workplace but of what Northrop Frye calls the educated imagination. It is this quality of mind that mainly divides the writer from the worker. Most commonly it comes from university, but it can be achieved at home too. Frye of course thinks it's great, but others have described it as being "de-educated," and I found out what that meant when I went back to work after five years of college. It was like being eight years old again and having to learn everything my father ever taught me about the concrete reality of work all over. It was worse than that, because I now had this abstract habit of mind I had to fight.

Participants in After the Shift mostly disagreed with White, feeling that his comments ignore the wide variation in levels of interest in the arts found in the workplace today. Sandy Shreve described her relation to an audience by saying she writes first to set down what she wants to say, in a form she feels comfortable using. Then her aim is to show her writing *both* to her workmates and to the non-work-oriented writers and editors of the mainstream literary world.

How schools and the media impede work literature from finding a larger audience was also discussed. The absence of an accurate consideration of daily work in school curricula helps teach that work is not a fit subject for critical examination, as well as not a fit subject for the arts. Schools and the media also indicate, by whom they direct attention to, that only certain occupations in society have the right to speak out. The words of employers, managers, politicians, and so on are treasured above the words of those whose lives will be affected by the decision the authorities make. Artists are seen as primarily coming from, and speaking to, the group of significant individuals in a community. "Good" artistic form and content is selected by this significant group out of all the possibilities presented to it by the artists. The "good" art is then assigned a high monetary worth, is enshrined in school curricula, and public endorsement of this choice is sought by means of a barrage of official praise for it in schools and the media.

Work writing, on the other hand, states that every job has importance in society and that whoever does that work is an expert concerning the value of this work and how this work affects individual and community existence. Therefore each of us has the right to speak out and be listened to, irrespective of financial status. The present educational and critical apparatus is not likely to devote a sustained effort to promoting this message.

Concerning the issue of familiar versus unfamiliar form, speakers at After the Shift noted that where the bulk of the population clings to a belief in the cultural forms of a previous era, there is usually a reason. One example of this behaviour is the popularity of traditional rhymed and metred verse compared to contemporary poetry. Although school leaves most people feeling inadequate in their grasp of the arts, one area of expertise an individual can be sure of is that poetry rhymes and has metre. After all, this is how poetry has been presented from nursery rhymes on through high school English classes. But if a person is subsequently confronted by the idea that, instead, poetry is created by means of careful selection of diction, rhythms, and line breaks, or by some other aspect of speech or writing, a negative reaction is likely. The new concept takes away from people the little they are sure they know about this art form. The new concept suggests, as school originally did (and as the media continue to insist), they are ignorant and misinformed about the arts.

One idea expressed at After the Shift for combating this situation calls for more sensitivity on the part of authors to others' attempts at writing. Throughout the work force, as in the population at large, many people try their hand at writing whether or not they intend to publish. More opportunities are needed for interaction between experienced writers and beginners or those who write in isolation from contemporary authors and literature. This interaction should include both face-to-face encouragement of new writers' developing skills and also increased availability of work literature by means of new, nonliterary venues for performance and publication.

The fourth issue raised at After the Shift concerned self-definition. As posed by Glen Downie, the question is: "When is a work writer not a work writer?" Does the adoption of a different subject matter, or of styles and techniques that move away from realistic narrative, mean an author has ceased to be a work writer?

VIWU had already grappled with this question internally, since none of its members limits her or his writing to workplace themes. The organization concluded that whereas the group's primary interest is work writing, individual members (in the words of a VIWU document on membership) "may be primarily interested in other writing forms at times."

But is work writing a "form," a genre, or a subject matter? The consensus at After the Shift was that work writing is essentially a point of view affecting whatever an author writes: the belief in work's importance because of its effect on our lives.

Mark Warrior defined this viewpoint as opposed to the prevailing ideology in society, including in the arts. Calling the ruling ideology "aristocratic," he said it argues that those who produce the world's goods and services are unimportant compared to the value of employers, managers, and even the right sort of artists. Literature that contains the artistocratic attitude, Warrior said, "really goes back to a sort of Platonic ideal which is those who produce in society are worthless, useless, and should only exist to keep those people going who actually do things which are valuable. And that is write, govern . . . create art of a certain kind."

Literature that incorporates the countervailing ideology, such as work writing, proposes that those who do the work of the world are important since our efforts each day create the society in which everyone lives. "That's the point of view I bring to all my writing," Warrior said. "And I would hope that no matter how the ways in which I earn my living might change, that point of view would remain there: that I see the value of all of us in helping create this world."

The final issue considered at After the Shift was the identification of tangible ways to increase the audience for work literature. While it was generally agreed that building an audience for this kind of writing is related to changes in society, work writers are not inclined to wait passively for a more supportive cultural environment.

A freewheeling discussion touched on many possible projects and activities aimed at reaching a larger audience. Among these is the production of a video on the work writing movement, to speak to people who ordinarily obtain their information about the world in ways other than reading. Increased publication of work writing in nonliterary periodicals, such as union or professional journals, was seen as important in acquainting more of the authors' co-workers with this material. Performances in nontraditional places, such as parks, and possibly combined with work-oriented music, would also extend public awareness of work literature's existence. Book tables at labour conventions, and hosting a labour film series combined with a lobby book table, were other suggestions discussed. As a means to encourage the appearance of more work writers, suggestions were made to conduct manuscript evaluation sessions for new writers during the year and to provide open-mike sessions at VIWU-sponsored readings.

New efforts to acquaint high school teachers and students with work writing were proposed. Among these were the circulation of a letter and brochure about VIWU to area high school English departments and librarians, with the offer to perform in schools.

Increased involvement in the literacy movement, especially work-place literacy programmes, was also deemed useful.

How many of these projects will ever be realized depends in part on the amount of energy the work writers can bring to the challenge of widening and deepening their audience. Whether these projects *would* significantly expand the audience for work writing also remains a question. But the present cultural environment will probably continue to spur such efforts, VIWU members concluded. Once anyone becomes conscious of the absence of the subject of daily work in our culture, it is difficult to return to a state of willful blindness.

New Jersey construction engineer and work anthropologist Herb Applebaum, in a paper written for Split Shift, sums up the current situation and the prospects for change:

> American and Canadian culture, dominated as it is by large corporations, huge bureaucracies and mass media profit seek-ers, will generate a literature which fosters escapism, consum-erism and sensationalism, all of which divert people's attention from social issues. Literature which deals with real lives, with working lives, will only find a market at the fringes. . . . Work literature stresses the collectivity of people and the importance of community, and as such, is a valued sector in our common culture, even if it is opposed by those in authority. . . .
>
> The gatekeepers of culture presume that the public prefers escapist themes, violent plots and one dimensional character-types. However, public apathy toward literature and reading suggests the public find little to relate to with regard to their own experiences. . . . An alternative culture, working-class cul-ture or work culture, certainly exists as a way of life. Writing about work, to date, is still only meager and fragmentary. Much of it is to be admired. But it has yet to become a real alternative to the cultural products presently on the market. . . . The fate of a book depends upon critics, distributors and self-appointed censors occupying positions of authority in publishing houses

and magazines and most of these consider work as an unworthy subject for literature. . . .

Consumerism and the subjects of love, death and nature are all safe subjects which will not shake up the social fabric. Writing about work and working lives faces an uphill battle. But it is an enterprise worth striving for.

9 SITTING BY THE GRAVE OF LITERARY AMBITION: WHERE I AM NOW IN MY WRITING

I discovered my forties to be a height of land from which I could gaze back down the route I had travelled and simultaneously peer ahead to consider future roads. I found that this assessment of where I had been and where I might go provoked a drastic increase in my level of emotional anxiety. The source of my extreme agitation was the realization that the paths that led most directly forward from those I was following were not likely to provide me much joy or pleasure. Struggling with this knowledge, I felt as if a load had shifted horribly in my life, as though a heavy weight in a backpack I carried had unexpectedly toppled sideways, forcing me off balance. After much frantic reeling around, and receiving assistance from friends and a few wisdom books, I started to understand that nearly all my behaviours — the conduct that brought me to my present moment of realization — had been picked up on the fly as I raced through infancy, childhood, adolescence, and my twenties and thirties.

I refer to behaviours in the plural because I began to comprehend that my conduct in any situation was the result of a web of interconnected responses developed as a consequence of events in my past, for good or ill. For instance, one legacy of my childhood is a fear of angry confrontation, since I retain the belief that rage directed at me will result in my physical or emotional annihilation. This belief led me as an adult to act in ways designed to minimize the possibility of having to face the anger of anyone close to me.

The consequence of such behaviours is that friends universally consider me "a nice guy." But in intimate relationships — where confrontation is inevitable, and where, in fact, confrontation is *required* for the relationship to grow and progress — I tried to hide my own anger and to deflect the anger of others through a number of techniques that proved highly destructive of intimacy and commitment over time.

Such adopted behaviours included my artistic practices as well as my patterns of interaction with other people. Because of my particular background, and especially my eagerness to take part in the social struggles of my historical era, I had devoted virtually no time to a consideration of what such acquired behaviours might mean in the long term. Yet the perspective available to me because of entering middle age revealed that very few of my behaviours had produced the results I wanted when I adopted them.

Recognizing this failure meant reevaluating my life as a writer. It is true that to an outsider I probably seem as successful as any Canadian poet of my generation. I have published ten collections of my poems with good national and regional publishers. My poems appear steadily in recognized literary periodicals in Canada and, unlike hardly any of my peers, in the United States (where I have no "reputation," and hence the poems must stand solely on their own merit). I have had more than my share of grants, awards, readings, media attention. My poems are reprinted both in Canadian and U.S. teaching anthologies. There is an individual entry on me in the latest edition of Mel Hurtig's *The Canadian Encyclopedia*. Because of my anthologies of, and essays about, contemporary literature about daily work, I have a readily identifiable niche in the world of letters. And a number of side benefits accrue for me from this interest in the new work writing, including recognition as an author among some groups and individuals ordinarily distant from literary concerns.

But from within that personality known as Tom Wayman, my new focus showed failure upon failure in connection with my writing. For more than twenty years I had worked obsessively, to the detriment of large areas of my emotional and social life, in pursuit of certain literary objectives. Now I had to conclude that none of these goals had been obtained, and that my artistic behaviours would *never* lead to the achievement of my aims.

My literary ambitions included the intent to help create a wider audience for poetry. I felt that clear speaking about everyday life, combined with humour, could regain an audience lost to poetry — lost because of the use of poetry as an instrument of torture in mass public education, and because of the accompanying academic attitude that regards the poet as a member of an artistic elite speaking to select individuals initiated into esoteric mysteries. Furthermore, I wanted to bring to this newly broadened audience for literature an artistic consideration of daily employment (the governing aspect of existence, after all, for most of our species). In turn, from such recognition of everyday work as a previously absent major theme in art, I desired a critical examination by people of the conditions of their own jobs. Here my belief was that such a consideration inevitably would lead to an awareness of the need to democratize the hours we are employed.

Besides these *social* ambitions for my writing, I looked to my poems to provide me with *personal* self-validation. Success as a writer meant that I had worth as a human being; setbacks or rejections meant a lowering of my self-esteem. In addition, I could defend my wish for the various trappings of artistic success — positive reviews, critical attention, invitations to read or speak, recognition of myself as someone of cultural importance — by regarding these as methods of bringing my artistic and social messages to the widest possible public. Artistic achievement was also intended to be a hedge against death: personal oblivion was less threatening if at least those tiny parts of my personality encoded as poems would live on.

Such ambitions for my writing were supposed to justify the behaviours I had adopted in order to realize these goals. The ends, then, were to justify the means. Yet at the moment when I could ruthlessly evaluate past conduct, I became aware that every dimension to my ambitions was doomed. It is not that I reject the social goals I held for my art; I simply had to acknowledge that I cannot achieve these aims by proceeding as before. And I had to admit that

I have no idea how these goals could be realized. Similarly I saw that by clinging to my old artistic behaviours I would never accomplish the *personal* ambitions I wished my writing to provide. My structures of artistic belief and behaviour collapsed.

In the midst of this turmoil, occurring concurrently with an equally devastating evaluation of goals in other areas of my life, I became the Squire of "Appledore," an estate near Nelson in the Selkirk Mountains of southeastern B.C. On my new property, in a front meadow between the house and the lane, I found a curious construction. A thin concrete foundation, which I later learned had once supported a chicken coop, outlines a rectangular space about the size of a large grave. The former owners of the estate used the area within the concrete border as a flower bed, so when I took possession of the property this space was heaped with marigolds, snapdragons, zinnias, daisies, gazanias, lobelias . . . all adding to the tomblike effect.

Standing beside these blossoms in the mountain sunlight, I knew at once what was buried within. Here is my Grave of Literary Ambition. The grave now boasts a tombstone I ordered prepared: "R.I.P. LITERARY AMBITION 1966-89." The dates respectively signify the year of my entry into a graduate writing programme, and hence the start of my formulation of aims for my art, and the year when the impossibility of my literary goals became absolutely evident to me. This spot is where I am now as a writer: sitting beside the Grave of Literary Ambition.

Yet I say I sit here "as a writer" because the burial of these literary ambitions in this place does not mean I have abandoned writing. Rather, I am trying now to pay attention to a more accurate sense of what my art can accomplish. My interest in pursuing my art, my social convictions, even my artistic techniques, all remain largely unchanged. But what I expect my writing to achieve in the world, and what I expect my writing to do for me, have considerably altered.

First of all, I am attempting to be vigilant that my writing no longer negatively interferes with my conduct as a human being. For I am aware now that each of us lives our lives as *people,* and not as artists — no more than as stockbrokers or fashion models or television repairpersons or drywallers. Where our work adversely affects our own daily lives — for instance, if it lessens the quality of our relations with other human beings (our family, friends, community) — the supposed necessity or nobility of that work in no way excuses such conduct harmful to ourselves or others.

For example, I no longer regard myself "only as good as the last book." In fact, my goodness or badness is not measurable in terms of the qualities (or quantities) of literary production. Similarly I do not want to be discouraged or upset by negative reviews, or by failure to obtain this grant or that literary award, or by exclusion from a certain anthology, or by adulation given to another writer. Such behaviour now seems to me identical to excessive reliance by anyone — artist or not — on external validation for a sense of worth. As writers, we have been encouraged by many things — not least a Romantic notion of the artist as someone consumed by her or his art — to substitute literary criticism for clear thinking about our behaviours as human beings. Yet from my vantage point in my forties, I believe no one can exist as complete men and women by behaving as solitary, driven practitioners of any occupation or skill. And if art is not to be limited to a record of human pathology, I am convinced it must be the product of whole, self-aware women and men.

My expectations of how my writing should interact with its audience have also shifted. Previously, when people told me of poems of mine they posted on a notice board at work, or when a couple once told me that reading aloud my love poems played an important part in their courtship, I thought these were simply nice, supplementary appendages to my literary career. Now I consider these uses of my writing to be the *most* significant publication my poems could have. A friend once told me how she, in acute emotional distress, retreated alone to a mountain wilderness. There, day after day, she sat beside a single flower. Eventually she understood from her contemplation of that alpine blossom that the same spark of life exists in the plant as in herself. She gained perspective, comfort, courage, and more from the experience. I would be very pleased if my poems from time to time provided other people with what this friend obtained from that wildwood flower.

Let me emphasize that I do not consider this a social *ambition* for my writing, however. That is, I do not write with this goal in mind. The social function I now want my art to perform arises from a personal need to articulate how it feels to be alive during that portion of history given me to live, to help create. What use my poems might possibly be to other people I now believe is beyond my control or concern.

What I hope to gain *personally* from my writing, beyond fulfilling my need to record my times, I find best articulated by another friend, the California poet Dennis Saleh. In his forties Saleh carefully examined his considerable publication record, as well as the grants, awards, publications, and critical acclaim he has *not* received.

Saleh said he questioned himself as to whether the absent aspects of his writing career were what he really needed. He concluded they were not. "What a writer needs most of all are *words,*" he said. "And I have plenty of words." By this he meant literally that he has a large and comprehensive vocabulary and command of grammar, with the ability to expand and adapt both to match whatever literary endeavours he undertakes. He also meant "words" metaphorically in the sense of ideas, projects, ongoing creative literary work that is meaningful and exciting to him. If Van Gogh scarcely sold a painting in his lifetime, but produced to the best of his abilities, surely that is a better model for us as writers than someone who, through a combination of chance, fashion, or geographic locale, has been anointed the current star in the tiny firmament of contemporary poetry. Thus, what today I ask of my writing to provide me is that it continue to reveal rich veins of ideas for me to pursue. And I want the exercise of my art in following these veins to help me master the appropriate literary techniques to extract, concentrate, and smelt this mental ore into a product that — at least to me — is vibrant, accurate, convincing. Again I do not see this wish as an ambition; my request is more a hope that I will continue to enjoy what I feel has been available for me up to the present.

Yet although I sit by the Grave of Literary Ambition, my commitment to certain forms and content in my writing has not changed. With regard to form I remain convinced of the need to craft poetry that speaks openly, accessibly, about contemporary social and personal conditions. I do not wish to add to the mysteries of human life, but rather to report back to as many in my community as possible what I have discovered about existence. After nearly thirty years of reading poetry, I am still intrigued with and impressed by the potential power of compression, of the resonant ambiguities sometimes found in English words and syntax, and of new possibilities for understanding generated by fresh approaches to conveying time or thought or viewpoint in writing. But I remain unconvinced of any *innate* advantage in obscurity, confusion, or difficult referentiality. I believe every poet needs to consider the status of the genre itself, as well as her or his artistic or personal needs. In a time of dwindling readership for all literary forms, I am convinced that any literary or careerist advantages in creating obstacles to a reader's understanding of a poem must be weighed against poetry's need not to discourage and turn away those men and women excluded by such obstacles from enjoyment of the art.

Also, I have observed that any development in art that erects a wall of difficult access between itself and a generally educated public quickly produces a social hierarchy. A group that considers itself an artistic elite begins to form and function, generally praising its own members for their appreciation and understanding of what to the uninitiated is gibberish or ugliness. Whether that elite consists solely of the artists, or includes the teachers, critics, and students parasitic on the creators of the art, this group rapidly adopts the aggressive behaviours all defensive human personalities and organizations practise. Which is sad, since the original motive for this development in art was probably not aggression but a sincere belief that aspects of human experience could better be depicted through new means.

But, to me, this unfortunate progression confirms a characteristic of elites, a characteristic I am convinced of by occurrences in my life and by my readings of history. Social and artistic elites, despite any rhetoric they may employ, are never the friends of the human race. How could a group interested in distancing themselves from the majority of their species ever offer a true benefit to those they despise? The greater the gap between the daily lives and concerns of elites and those of the majority — that is, the less the elite understands about how the majority regards and copes with existence — the more likely any solutions proposed by the elite for the problems facing the majority will be quixotic at best and harmful or destructive at worst. This awareness is another reason why I retain my wish to write as clearly as possible about what seems to me worth setting down. I do not want my skills with language to separate me from my neighbours, but to facilitate an exchange of information and ideas between us.

The other formal quality besides clarity that I wish to keep unchanged in my poems is the presence of narratives. I believe all literature begins with storytelling, the identical impulse that fuels gossip, shoptalk, and many other human linguistic interactions. A literary form that abandons the narrative seems to me very far from home, easily diverted into unproductive byways and dead ends. For me the hunger for story is part of being human, and goes a long way to explain why people can display more interest in the biography of certain authors than in their literary productions, or why when men and women glance through most current literary periodicals or anthologies, such readers can find themselves turning to scan the contributors' notes rather than continuing to peruse the literary artifacts.

In terms of content I retain my fervent conviction of the need to bring into literature an accurate portrayal of the conditions and effects of contemporary daily work. Of course, this subject is not the only one that interests me, as my previous books attest. Nor do I believe that the theme of work is the only important one for art. But to portray human behaviour in literature as though it were not shaped and governed by daily labour — in short, not to depict the details of everyday employment — is to limit seriously art's ability to explore and comment on human existence. And the *cumulative* effect of making daily work a taboo subject in our cultural world, as well as in our entertainment and educational worlds, is to distort grotesquely the image humanity presents to itself. The burning secret hidden by the taboo — the lack of freedom at work everywhere on the planet — sears and scars men and women. Here the majority of us live half free and half obedient to arbitrary authority. I cannot help but observe how much the distemper and discontent of our place and era is rooted in this bizarre existence, where we are expected to alternate every few hours between being freedom-loving, responsible citizens of a democratic community while off the job, and docile, unquestioning respecters of authority while at work. To me it is not surprising that a majority of writers — like a majority of citizens — would rather look at *anyone* else's problems, or our own problems in *any* other sphere of everyday life, than tackle the core issue of our daily existence: the need to liberate ourselves at the heart of the day.

Artists sometimes feel they have escaped the cage of daily waged or salaried employment if they can survive economically through selling their art or their artistic knowledge. But as Abraham Lincoln, among others, pointed out, no community can survive partly enslaved and partly free. Even if you and I succeed in finding or creating nonhierarchically managed employment for ourselves, we live surrounded by women and men who do not enjoy this privilege. And it is among these people — including our relatives, children, friends — that we must spend our time on this planet. Not until all are free are any of us disentangled from the undemocratic chains and cables that contemporary work tightens around the members of our community. And we will never build Paradise with slave labour.

Despite my efforts to help swing the searchlight of art to shine on this enormous blacked-out area of our lives, I realize only a few now writing besides myself see this topic as a priority. For the immediate future, contemporary poetic content will largely consist of ahistorical landscapes and still lifes, sexual narcissism, Third Worldism, the assumption of voices impossibly removed from the author's experiences, idealistic philosophies, pseudo-science, and more.

Yet the delight I find in continuing to map the possibilities of the inclusion of daily work in literature — as well as other themes — is the happiness any explorer feels, whether or not a new land is judged attractive or significant by stay-at-homes. More tangibly, from time to time I encounter a writer or book that presents in an especially accomplished manner the subjects or approaches that are most meaningful to me. These discoveries provide me with the same excitement I feel when a folksong group launches into a tune where for once the form and content and performance are all complementary, all describing and illuminating some vital part of the human story. For a few moments I have a sense of the musicians as a well-tuned engine, powerfully and smoothly propelling the room of women and men onward at an exhilarating pace towards a fuller, more satisfying life. To me this is art at its best. And my joy at encountering such achievement is completely unconnected to any ambition, except that events like this serve as a reminder of why I love words and what words can do.

So I sit at the Grave of Literary Ambition, but with my earlier commitment to writing and to specific forms and content intact. Yet when I replanted the Grave this past spring, I put mainly annuals into its soil. I meant by this cultivation of plants that will die within the year to honour how change implies death — the end of one possibility for whatever has changed. For although death diminishes, it also clears the ground for new growth, new developments, always with the possibility of improvement in what comes next. And the recognition of my own eventual death is part of what impels me to take stock of my life from time to time. Thus, the withering of the plants each fall in the Grave of Literary Ambition also honours that ultimate judgement of myself and my behaviours.

From this place in the middle of my life I feel I can still cover great distances, cross many rivers, journey through much even and uneven territory before dark. But the self-evaluation I am undergoing suggested to me the need to pause, to hold still for a while to properly bury and commemorate my dead. To discard hastily the ambitions that were an important part of my life for many years, to toss them away like garbage and quickly press on, would discredit not only them but myself — the self they helped evolve to the point where they were not needed. Whatever time I have left, whatever directions I go from here, I will return each spring I can to replant this Grave. To me it is both wellspring and river mouth, tomb and cradle. I look forward to seeing what will grow from it.